MW01087746

Serpent of Old

By

TR Pearson

A novel

Barking Mad Press
2019

Publisher's Note: This is a work of fiction. Names, characters, places, and incidents are a product of the author's imagination. Locales and public names are sometimes used for atmospheric purposes. Any resemblance to actual people, living or dead, or to businesses, companies, events, institutions, or locales is completely coincidental.

Serpent of Old/TR Pearson
ISBN 978-1-7927264-0-8

Once you've found yourself high in the limbs of a cedar with the tree squirrels and the mayflies hoping a gal on the ground doesn't look up and shoot you with your own rusty gun, you're probably overdue for a fresh evaluation of your choices. I was parked and puckered because I'd done a favor for a neighbor, a boy with a talent for messes that never seemed to stick to him. Whenever Ronnie made the mischief, somebody else usually lost the teeth.

A widow lived in Ronnie's house when I moved onto the street. Then she died and her daughter sold the place to a sketchy speculator who hired Ronnie to work improvements, but he chiefly piddled and drank, slept on a rollaway bed in the front room and lived out of a sack. Once that speculator had bugged out ahead of a raft of bank fraud charges, Ronnie claimed the house in lieu of payment. He didn't file papers or anything, just declared the place was his, and nobody came around to pitch him out.

My girlfriend at the time detested Ronnie because he'd called her big-boned, and she didn't like the way

I'd wave and shout at Ronnie, "Hey." Of course, by then she already had a couple of guys on the side where she worked and another one she carried on with at the homewares store. And I do mean *at* the homewares store. Those two got found out in the break room by a chatty girl from plumbing who went wide with what she'd seen, so I just kept on waving, kept on telling Ronnie, "Hey."

Gail left a note on our battered hoosier when she finally moved out of the house. It was chiefly a list of the ways I'd let her down. She'd roped one of her new boyfriends into helping her haul her stuff, and Ronnie watched them at it from his glider. I came home to that cabinet, three dinner plates, and a couple of ladderback chairs.

Ronnie told me Gail had stood in our yard calling him nasty things.

"Got a mouth on her," he informed me and then, "Rollaway's yours if you want it." Ronnie had graduated by then to a mattress on the floor.

I took the loan of that bed and dragged it home. It proved to be all he needed.

"Might be wanting you for a thing or two," was how Ronnie chose to put it. Then he winked, I remember, and stuck his tongue through the gap where an incisor used to be.

If you asked him, Ronnie would tell you he was a

handyman and sometimes painter, but in truth, he was primarily a thief. I'll give him this, he was fairly conscientious about his stealing. He'd relieve folks of things they weren't taking care of, stuff they'd left out in the weather and seemed indifferent to. Neglect, for Ronnie, was a sign and a signal, an unspoken invitation for him to come in the night and make off (say) with your garden tiller because the best you could do was half cover the motor with a rusty tub.

To pay him back for the loan of the rollaway, I drove Ronnie out to a farm where he'd heard about a step van in a pecan grove doing nobody any good. He directed me north past the river and well off the blacktop into the boonies, down a weedy track and onto a spread that appeared to be long abandoned. Both of the barns were half collapsed, and the farmhouse chimney was in the yard. The cow lots and the pastures were choked with scrub and well on their way to woodland.

That pecan grove was up a hillside with a view of three junked tractors, but the panel truck Ronnie had come for wasn't close to ruined itself. The tires had air enough to drive on, and the thing looked lately painted, even if poorly and with a roller. You could see the old logo underneath from back when it was a laundry truck—a little round man in a cap and bow tie carrying a bundle of shirts.

Ronnie turned up the ignition key in a console cubby, and the battery had charge enough to crank. The engine caught once I'd pulled off the blower and cleaned out some acorn hulls.

"You sure about this?" I asked him. "It's Whelan country back in here."

Those Whelans were also thieves, but they were more in the way of marauders. They didn't go in for conscientious and had a ferocious feral streak. I figured there were two or three dozen of them between us and the blacktop, and it seemed certain to me they'd think that truck was theirs.

"Worked it out already," was what Ronnie said.

I knew that had to be a lie since nobody on this green earth worked stuff out with Whelans. Instead of calling him on it, though, I just gave Ronnie a healthy head start and fully expected to find his carcass on my way back to the main road. I ended up driving past the usual Whelan mess and Whelan squalor. Grown Whelans gave me the stink eye from their trashy yards while their nasty children fooled around in the dirt. A few Whelan mongrels chased me, and a Whelan goat in the ditch quit chewing on fence wire long enough to glance my way and pee.

I found Ronnie at home on his glider enjoying a butt and a beer. He'd parked that step van across the road in our neighbors' driveway. They'd RV'd out to Omaha to visit their grandchildren. Casper and Janet were big on traveling this world in their camper van, which Casper worked to make less roadworthy year to year. Janet would own up to having felt a little crowded and constricted, so Casper would add an alcove or a wing.

"Meaning to keep it?" I asked Ronnie.

He shook his head. "Got a boy who needs it for hauling sheetrock." Ronnie motioned for me to follow him across the road to Casper's driveway. "Ask you something?" He flung open the back bay doors. "Think I ought to hose her out?"

I recognized the stink immediately. Something had aged in there and rotted, but that bay looked clean enough except for a stain on the sheet-metal floor about the size of a paint can lid. It had some gritty patches and what looked like sprigs of fur, but I knew Ronnie wasn't after me for an honest forensic assessment. He just wanted to hear not to bother with the hose.

His buyer came around the next afternoon in a low-slung LeSabre. He was riding with a buddy, and they were each wearing a coat of compound dust. That boy inspected the truck for maybe two minutes before him and Ronnie set into dickering over the don't-have-a-title price. The guy kept pulling cash from his pocket. It was balled up and unsorted. He'd smooth bills out against his thigh, hand a few to Ronnie, and then they'd do fresh math and dicker a little more.

I was watching from my front room when they finally struck a deal. That sheetrocker gave the high sign, and his buddy drove off in the Buick. He followed him soon enough up our road in his brand new truck, and it was three days later exactly when the lady cop came knocking. Once she couldn't raise Ronnie, she swung over to call on me.

I was lurking in the front hall. "Saw you in the window," she shouted, so there wasn't much for it but to open up.

She was a looker, this woman, and couldn't undo it, though she was certainly giving it a go. She wasn't wearing any makeup that I could see, and she'd piled her hair up in a straggly ball that she'd run through with a ballpoint pen, one of those cheap Bics she'd gnawed flat. She had on the sort of shirt and pants you'd work coliseum parking in, and her shoes looked padded in an orthopedic way. She'd jotted stuff on her left hand that had survived the humidity poorly. On her right wrist, she wore two grimy braids of yarn, both of them brown.

She pointed at Ronnie's house. "Know where he is?"

I shook my head. There was a decent chance Ronnie was up to grand larceny somewhere.

"What's your name?"

I told her. She plucked her pen out of her bun and made a note on her palm.

"Cop, right?"

She showed me her platinum badge and her county ID. Edita Ruiz.

"He got a job?" She glanced at Ronnie's house.

"Handyman stuff," I told her.

"When did you last see him?"

"Yesterday maybe."

Ruiz reminded me of a girl I'd dated one time back in high school if a date can be her getting drunk at a football game and her girlfriends drafting me to drive her home. She'd been seeing a boy who played in the backfield, but they'd had a squabble, and she'd gone and consoled herself with a pint of rum. I was sober and available and had come to the game in my daddy's powder-blue Fairlane.

I did stop on the way a couple of times but just so she could lean out and spew. At her house, she patted me on the head and called me pookie or something before flopping onto a patio settee and passing out for good. I very nearly covered her with my jacket but decided I was too fond of it for that. I'm afraid I stood there and watched her sleep for longer than was seemly. Even drooling and smelling of vomit she still seemed awfully fine.

"What do you do?" Ruiz asked me.

"I cook at Double D's. Work some framing when they need me. Drive a school bus sometimes."

Then she wanted to know if I knew a man. She said his full name twice. "His friends called him Tito. Sheetrocker." She showed me a picture of him on her phone. "Found this in his wallet." She pulled from her trouser pocket a plastic bag with what looked like a scrap of envelope in it. Ronnie's address was scrawled in pencil on the thing.

"Could be Ronnie knows him," I told her. "That boy in some sort of trouble?"

"Not anymore. He's about ten kinds of dead." She grabbed my hand and wrote her phone number right across my palm. "You have him call me."

I gave her assurances I would and then heard Ronnie's hinges squeaking before she was even off the street.

"What did she want?"

"Your sheetrocker bought it."

"My what?"

"Guy with the truck."

"What happened to him?"

"Don't know." I showed him my hand. "Left her number for you."

He didn't call it straightaway but decided instead to enlist his professional girlfriend. He'd worked out an arrangement with her which allowed him to pay her in liquor and the odd carton of smokes. That way their relationship felt less like commerce to Ronnie, which he far preferred because he had a touch of romance in his soul.

I never knew the woman's actual name since Ronnie only called her Sugar, would often sing it out when she'd get up to something 'professional' in the house. Ronnie put Sugar onto finding out about this dead sheetrocker since he knew she was friendly in a regular way with Deputy Ike. Ike worked chiefly at the middle school where he wandered the hallways being armed and winded. It turned out he'd heard from his deputy buddies that this Tito had gotten beat to death with a brick.

"Flat tore up," Sugar told Ronnie. "Busted all to pieces." According to Sugar, they'd found him stuck head-first out in a mud hole somewhere. "Like a fencepost," was how she put it, and that was enough to get Ronnie upset. He couldn't conceive of the scoundrel who'd go to such bother for a sheetrocker.

"Call that lady cop," was my ongoing advice. "You know she'll just come back."

Ronnie's impulse, naturally, was to tell the police some made-up story. "I was selling a mower, and he come round to see it. Didn't buy it. Just looked and took off."

Then he insisted I go with him on his visit to the PD because, apparently, rollaway bed debt is kind of a bottomless thing.

On the way, Ronnie worked out more details. "Let's say a Snapper," he told me, "and I was wanting eighty-five firm."

"Seems low for a Snapper."

"Bent back axle. Blade's dinged up. Like that."

"Now," I told him, "it seems a little high."

Our local police had lately moved into a big, old building downtown where a bank had been with pneumatic tubes and teller cages and marble. It was a temporary thing until their regular spot got rebuilt and repaired. A local lady in a snit over a trash bin citation had left the sheriff's parking lot at high speed in the wrong direction, which had put her in the lobby instead of out in the street.

We found Edita Ruiz standing at one of those tables where you'd fill out your deposit slip back in the day.

She saw us coming. "This him?" she asked me of Ronnie.

I nodded, and Ronnie told her, "I was selling a Snapper" instead of maybe "Hello."

She led us into a temporary room they'd closed off in a corner. There was a picnic table in it and two stacks of traffic cones.

"You run an ad?" she asked.

Ronnie shook his head. "Sign on it. Eighty-five firm."

"So Mr. Richards just ... happened by?"

Ronnie did some squinting.

"Walter Elsworth Richards," she told him. "Tito, now deceased." She showed us Tito's driver's license. A full year expired, I noticed.

"Yes, ma'am," Ronnie told her. "Offered sixty, but like I said I was eighty-five firm."

"So why do you think he had your address?" She showed Ronnie the sack with the scrap of envelope in it.

"Can't say."

"You sure you didn't know this man?"

She was giving us plenty of chances to do the square and honest thing, but that sort of business is usually down the road a ways for Ronnie. He'll get to the truth when nothing else will work.

"No ma'am," Ronnie said.

"How about you?" she turned my way.

I shook my head.

For some reason, Ronnie decided just then to tell her, "Hear he's all tore up."

"Oh yeah? Who from?"

"Girl I know. She might have got it from Ike."

Deputy Ike was notorious locally for rattling on about everything, so it was right and proper that Ruiz should mutter and snort.

"Stuck in a mud hole, wasn't he?" Ronnie just wouldn't quit.

Ruiz passed a moment thinking and then stood up and said, "Stay put." She left me and Ronnie in there with those stacks of traffic cones, and I took occasion to try to get Ronnie to cork up all his questions.

"That's how they get you," I told him.

"I'm cool," Ronnie said. He was always sure of himself for no solid reason. I'm more of a fretter and usually start out convinced I'm in the wrong.

Ruiz came back with a stack of photos that she laid out on the picnic table and then slid one over to us. "Yeah, they stuck him in the mud."

He was buried up past his hips, and his legs were poking straight up in the air. No trousers. No boots. Just tube socks and a couple of tattooed calves. Then we got to see a picture of Tito the dead sheetrocker laid out on a royal blue tarp.

"That's him. He come around." Ronnie slid the picture my way.

"Alone?"

"Might have had a boy in the car."

"Oh?"

"Gopher probably," Ronnie said and glanced my way.

"Didn't see him."

"Sure you did," Ronnie insisted and described the guy by way of a refresher. The stringy hair. The compound dust. "Driving a Buick. Gold."

Ruiz made a note on her hand and then shoved the rest of the photographs at us so we could look at them however we pleased. Pond shots. Dead guy shots. One closeup of the mud hole.

"Where is this?" Ronnie wanted to know.

Ruiz couldn't be bothered to say. "I'll call you if something comes up," she told us and stood so we'd do the same.

Out in the lot, Ronnie boasted about how slick he'd been with the woman and confessed he might romance her if he met with the chance sometime.

"Listen to me. I don't usually have no use at all for Mexicans." Then Ronnie lit a Merit, smoked it down in four or five tokes, and was in my car a nanosecond before he said, "Come on."

I find it hard to tell people I'm put out with them in anything like real time, so I muttered at Ronnie later in my house alone. I made a pact with myself that I was at the end of my rollaway favors, but then Ronnie stole a limb lopper and gave it to me as a gift, so we were properly friendly again by the time that panel truck came back.

I was leaving my house in the morning dark for my shift at Double D's when I saw it across the road in Casper's driveway. The back bay doors were standing open, and I could see underneath the paint the little fat man in the bow tie with the bundle of folded shirts. On the spot, I decided Ronnie had gone out and stolen that truck again, and I was about to march over and bang on his door to find out why he'd done it when he came outside in his undershorts and said, "You seeing this?"

He was as rattled as I was. We crossed the road together and eased up to the bumper from where we could see a dark smear on the inside bay wall.

It was maybe four feet long and looked like it had

been wiped there with a rag. Somebody had written in it before it dried, probably with a finger, and not a scrawl but letters like you might see on a fancy restaurant menu or one of those wedding invitations that comes in about eight parts.

"What does that even say?" Ronnie asked me.

I could make it out well enough, even knew where the words had come from because I've got history with the Good Book.

"Revelation," I told Ronnie. "Says 'Serpent of Old'."

2

My father was a preacher, tent revivals exclusively, and he was a hell of a Bible thumper and pentecostal zealot with a knack for making people feel sanctified and saved. Not so much us back home. I remember him beating me once with a chalice, which he insisted the Prince of Peace had called him to do.

When he met my mother, she was born again and authentically holy while he was a drinker and a fighter running around with a low crowd. He fell for her hard enough to drag himself to church three times a week, but it never took in any genuine way. The man had a head for scripture, and he was a powerful testifier, but that came with a violent temper and a weakness for Everclear.

He was a bad one for knocking my mother around, and he pawed at my sister a bit, so she got moved out of the house and put with a cousin. My mother wanted something like that for me but couldn't find a spot, which meant I stayed home and suffered with her through his fits and rages until she decided to bring them to an end.

He hadn't done anything in particular the day she helped him quit this earth. He was just out in the side yard fooling with his Fairlane. I was on the back porch getting our stove wood straight when I heard my mother call my father by his given name. That was peculiar because for some years he'd been using Caleb. It came with an Old Testament pedigree, and he'd decided it helped him pass as decent and God-fearing. His real name was Lawrence, and when I heard her say it a second time, I left the porch to find out what was up.

Daddy was giving her a dose of Ephesians, reminding her of her wifely duties, when she put two quick rounds in him and then a third one shortly after. Before I could reach her, he was on his knees telling her vile things.

She was using great-granddaddy's .45, a rusty Colt Peacemaker, and I guess she figured three was enough because she shoved the thing my way. Then my mother described in some detail the casserole she'd made for my supper and told me how to warm it up and what to eat it with. I could hear the first of the sirens by then. She'd called before she came outside.

He hung on for nearly a week, and there was talk of him pulling through, but our sweet Savior finally took him from us. My mother confessed her way into Goochland prison and has another six years yet. When I go to see her, she spends our time together apologizing because she knew from the first he was a bad seed but married him anyway.

I'm like my father in that I have a ready memory for Scripture and like my mother in that I ordinarily keep it to myself.

That wasn't going to work with Ronnie who kept asking, "What does it mean?"

So I quoted the whole verse to him since I knew it end-to-end. "And the great dragon was thrown down, the serpent of old called Satan and the Devil who deceives the world."

"What does *that* mean."

I pointed out Ruiz's sedan easing up the road. "If I was you, I'd go put on some pants."

I'd called the woman straightaway, and the idea was me and Ronnie would work out something to tell her about that truck before she came, but we'd squandered our time in quarreling over sexual politics because I said the writing looked to me like something a woman would do, and Ronnie got ill and chivalrous about it. He went around, for some reason, with a crazy high opinion of women, which seemed odd for a man who (more or less) paid one to roll around with him a couple of times a month.

Ruiz had brought a guy with her, and when he climbed out, she told us just, "Grimes." Then she encouraged Ronnie, with a look alone, to put on some damn trousers.

Grimes was short and thick, had a comb-over he appeared to have largely quit on, and he gave the immediate impression of not being worth a hot damn. He had a lot of attention to spare for the toothpick he was gnawing, but it took effort to get him to notice anything else.

"So?" Ruiz said my way. I walked her over to the step van and pointed out the smear on the back bay wall.

She made out the words well enough on her own. "Mean something to you?" she asked me. I quoted the entire verse, and Ruiz raised a weary noise like she'd heard all the New Testament she could stand.

"This his?" she pointed at Casper's house.

Because Ronnie and I hadn't settled on exactly what to say, the best I could come up with was, "They're in Omaha."

That prompted an additional weary noise from Ruiz, but she elected to leave me alone once she saw Ronnie running back across the road. He was wearing his usual grimy jeans and struggling with some kind of shirt that looked wrong even from over where we were. It proved to be one of Sugar's tube tops that Ronnie had grabbed by mistake. The thing had ruffles and spangles on it, was about the color of a Key West sunset, and Ronnie wore it briefly upside, long enough to give Grimes a hoot. Then he yanked it off and darted home again.

By that time, Grimes had done some thinking about

me and pointed his toothpick my way. "Gail, right?"

I pictured Grimes buying a toilet float and getting a juicy earful, but before I could spit out one thing or another, Ronnie came hustling back. It turned out he'd done a spot of thinking.

"Here's the thing," Ronnie said, and he told Ruiz all about the pecan grove and that step van sitting up there doing nobody any good. Then, having started in the middle, Ronnie veered to the beginning and acquainted Ruiz with the rollaway bed he'd lent me once my girlfriend cleaned me out.

Grimes went triumphant. "Knew it," he said and produced a fresh toothpick from his front shirt pocket by way of celebration.

"Never was a mower, right?" Ruiz didn't mess around. "And you two stole this truck, I'm guessing."

"Here's the thing," Ronnie told her. "We went out there fishing, me and him, and that truck was sitting around doing nobody any good."

I decided spontaneously to tell the woman the truth. I don't know why exactly. It just seemed like the sensible option.

"Wasn't any fishing," is how I started. "Went out there for the truck." Then I described the route we'd taken and what we'd done once we arrived there.

I enjoyed the sensation of feeling honest and at least quasi-upstanding. Not that I'm regularly a rascal like

Ronnie, but I cut corners too, and while I might not go around lying, I'm quick enough to withhold the truth. It felt far better than I would have guessed to speak to Ruiz without calculation, to just tell her what I remembered and not worry about how it might land.

I'd long been the cringey, reluctant sort who'd say as little as he could manage, the kind who'd end up on a rollaway bed because his girlfriends all had boyfriends, the sort to lead a life a fool like Grimes could openly sneer about.

"Sat two days right here." I pointed at Casper and Janet's driveway.

"They're actually in Nebraska?" she asked me.

I nodded. "When they go off, they give him a key." I confessed that for a good long while I'd been troubled and wounded by that since Ronnie never bothered to collect their mail or water their plants, and he fed Casper and Janet's cat by dumping Friskies out on the floor.

"Not how I'd do, but people seem to like Ronnie." Me and Ruiz together favored him with a moment of mystified study, enough to prompt Ronnie to ask both of us, "What?"

I gave her all I had on that dead sheetrocker and his buddy with the stringy hair. "Could be they knew of Ronnie, but he didn't know them." Then since Ruiz left me an opening for it, I decided to inform Grimes, "Gail got into my bank account and took just about all my money. If you're tied up with her, get untied and quick."

Grimes shifted his toothpick uneasily. Ronnie pointed at that panel truck and told us all, "It was sitting out there doing nobody any good."

A van turned onto our road, and Grimes waved it over to us. Inside was what passed with the local PD for a forensic team. An old guy and a girl who was probably thirty but looked like she was twelve while he was a shade of pale you rarely see off of a gurney. He lit a cigarette and smoked it down to the filter between the van and the panel truck. The girl carried all their forensic tools and both of their paper suits, and the old guy leaned against Casper and Janet's mailbox while she helped him into his outfit.

His name was Flynn and hers was something chirpy that nobody ever called her. Katie or Emma or Marcy Lou. She said it out loud just the once and then answered only to "Hey" and "You".

Ruiz waited until they'd started photographing and inspecting that step van before she told me and Ronnie she wanted us to take her to the pecan grove. Ruiz even called up Double D's and talked to Becky for me, explained to her why I'd probably miss my shift.

I could hear the racket of Becky's fury through the speaker of Ruiz's phone. Becky was buzzing like a carpenter bee up a borehole.

"No, a murder," Ruiz told her. "Going to be a while yet." Then she killed the call and said my way, "It's sounding like you're fired."

Becky fired everybody all the time. She was grumpy in a regular way and wore her jeans so tight that she often looked like a balloon animal. I told all of that to Ruiz once we were in her Ford sedan, and she found me in the rearview and said, "Noted."

Ronnie more or less sent her the way I would have gone, and on the trip out he floated the theory that the dead sheetrocker might have tangled with Whelans.

"Bad bunch, those boys," Ronnie declared.

Ruiz said, "Yeah, we know."

"Doesn't sound like them," was my assessment. "Those Whelans do everything in a damn rage." I couldn't see them digging a hole just to stuff a dead sheetrocker in it.

I caught Ruiz glancing my way in the rearview mirror like maybe I was getting a rethink from her, like I was moving the needle with my frank and honest talk.

Ronnie got us to the pipe gate where Ruiz had to stop and park because the rest of that track was far too washed out for a Grand Marquis. So we walked, and Ronnie pointed at every dilapidated thing to help establish all the ways that farm sure looked conspicuously abandoned. So how could anybody blame a guy for pinching a truck out there?

"He got family?" I asked of the dead sheetrocker.

"A dog and an ex-wife so far," Ruiz told me.

"Into drugs or something?"

She shook her head. "Not yet." Then she directed Grimes to find out from the county who owned the property, and he stopped walking and pulled his phone from his pocket, gave it a squinty, defeated look.

We kept on going, past the half-collapsed barns and the mildewed farmhouse with its stacked stone chimney in the yard. I let Ronnie do most of the talking and hung back slightly behind Ruiz so I could watch her from a spot where she couldn't easily see me.

"What did they dig his hole with?" Ronnie wanted to know.

"What would you dig it with?" she asked him.

"Mud or clay?"

"Some of both."

"Shovel maybe, if I had one, but you'd probably want some of those post-hole gizmos too."

Ruiz said back something in the vicinity of, "Hmm."

"Hit it, didn't I?" Ronnie asked her.

But she shook her head. "We're figuring they made him dig it with his hands."

I'd been thinking dead Tito must have gotten into a fix with a hardcore crew that made the occasional example of people like him. Softened them up with a brick first and then planted them out in the country meaning for the news of it to reach other folks who were in a fix as well.

"Got to be drugs," was my judgment on it.

That earned me a "Hmm" from Ruiz.

Ronnie led us up to the pecan grove, and he made sure Ruiz got a look at all the rusty tractor carcasses to help confirm that truck was up there doing nobody any good.

"Where'd y'all find him anyway?" I asked her.

She motioned for us to follow and then led us over a rise above what looked like a five-acre pond down in a swale a quarter mile at most from that pecan grove.

I think that's the moment me and Ronnie gave up on being entirely blameless. I remember saying something to Ruiz like, "Oh."

She made us walk down to the pond bank even though we weren't all that curious or eager, but Ruiz seemed convinced that a hole in the mud was something we needed to see as a possible consequence, I guess, of stealing panel trucks or borrowing rollaway beds or, maybe, having faithless girlfriends.

They'd made the usual cop mess down there—coffee cups, cigarette butts, and all variety of wrappers, along with a box half full of purple rubber gloves. There was yellow tape strung here and there, all of it shifting on the breeze, and a trio of for sale signs the cops had plucked from yards somewhere to stand on in the soft mud while they worked.

Ruiz walked us to the hole and made us look in. It was easily two feet deep and soupy at the bottom where the mud and the slop had mixed in with the blood.

"How'd you know that truck was out here?" Ruiz asked Ronnie mostly.

"This boy said he'd seen it," Ronnie told her. "I got him to tell me where."

"I'll need to talk to him."

Ronnie nodded. "It was just sitting out here," he told us both, "not doing anybody any good."

Ruiz turned my way "How about you? Anything to say?"

I'd dredged up a scrap of Proverbs that seemed particularly apt for the moment.

"Ill-gotten treasures," I said, "have no lasting value, but righteousness delivers us from death."

3

At Double D's I usually work with a guy named Rochelle. He's from some dust trap in Alabama, is large and black and strategically jolly because he's knocked around enough to know what'll help him get along. We take turns at the griddle and the dish sink and make everything the way Becky wants it. That means salty, a little greasy, but still bland.

Double D's clientele is chiefly geriatric, and most of them stand in opposition to flavor in their food.

Rochelle sings while he works. Gospel often. Some Peabo. The odd dash of Puccini, and occasionally current numbers he's heard in his car while driving in. We're Double D friends exclusively. I saw Rochelle in the Walgreen's once, and we ran out of chit chat in about a quarter minute. That's never a problem in the kitchen where Rochelle can just break into song.

"She find you yet?" was the first thing he asked me the morning after Ruiz.

I'd dodged Becky by coming in the back door, but she saw me through the service window and rolled in soon enough. I was treated to an earful about my duties and my obligations and then got unfired for the moment in a conditional way.

Since Rochelle was raised in a holiness church and knew even more Scripture than I did, I told him all about what had gone on, and he dipped into the Gospels and unfreighted himself of assorted hellish bits he knew by heart.

"Behold," Rochelle told me as kind of a capper, "I have set before you an open door, which no one is able to shut."

I was at the sink by then washing two days worth of dishes. That was your reward at Double D's for missing a shift, and Rochelle was on the griddle cooking flapjacks and sausage patties, four-egg omelets and bacon by the pound. I described what I'd heard and what I'd seen out on that farm with Ronnie and Ruiz. Then I told Rochelle about all the dark thoughts I'd grappled with in the night while trying to account for what that brand of carnage might actually mean.

"People," Rochelle told me, "get up to all kinds of mess."

"Plenty of Whelans around there," I said, "but it doesn't really sound like them."

I was aware Rochelle had a lively personal history with Whelans. Naturally, he had experience with the vast bulk of pinheads in the vicinity because they were all white and local and he was black and imported.

But I knew for a fact he'd tangled specifically with two Whelans at the firehouse where the crew was having a fish fry and Rochelle was delivering slaw. Becky had donated it partly because the squad had asked her to give them something and partly because it was borderline expired.

The firehouse was on Rochelle's way home, so he was just doing Becky a favor and had dropped off the slaw when a pair of Whelans stopped him in the parking lot. Somebody had given those boys fish fry tickets, and they'd come early to get their feed on but decided to have some giggles causing a Negro trouble first. Ordinarily, Rochelle would ignore that stuff, but those Whelans happened to catch him in a mood, and the way I heard it he snatched up the skinny one and clubbed the fat one with him and then kicked both of them around the parking lot for a pretty considerable while.

A trio of fire squad boys eventually weighed in on the Whelan side of things since, even if Whelans were abject trash, they also passed for Caucasian, and the whole business got wild and ugly enough to end up in front of a judge.

There were two battered Whelans, some scuffed up firefighters, nine civilians laid low by Becky's effervescent coleslaw, and one big black short-order cook from down by Tuscaloosa, so the magistrate was able to spread the blame around. Everybody got to pay a fine, and Rochelle spent four days at the sink.

"Or maybe," I suggested to Rochelle, "Whelans are into weird stuff now."

Whelans had long been known for stealing most anything they ran across and fighting especially Bigelows whenever their blood got up. Nobody (particularly Whelans) could remember why they did it, but they'd been battling Bigelows far too long to quit.

"Naw," Rochelle said.

"Somebody made that sheetrocker dig a hole," I told him. "They beat him with a brick and put him in it."

"Too many steps for Whelans," was Rochelle's view. "Those boys are one damn thing at a time."

I'd lived all my life in one or the other of two adjacent counties, so I felt like I had a fix on the moral limits of the place. A sheetrocker tenderized with a brick sure seemed like a corner turned.

"Don't like it," I told Rochelle.

He moved bacon around and grunted. "Tell you this. For damn sure this fool's white."

Becky came in with a chunk of eggshell some customer had found in a flapjack, so Rochelle got the sink for a while, and I went to the griddle in his place.

Double D's closes at two o'clock now. We used to stay open for supper until it became clear our clientele aren't the sort to drive at night. So I have afternoons free for a school bus route if one of the regulars can't make it, and I do grunt work for a contractor when he's got a house to build, but frequently I'm free to knock around.

I arrived home to find Ronnie had treated himself to a Sugar interlude. I could hear him warbling from over in my driveway. He's loud but quick, and that's probably why Sugar lets him get away with barter since sex with Ronnie can't put her out terribly much.

Sugar drives a Toyota that's more Bondo than not, and she goes around with a dog you could just about fit in a coffee can. His name's Tuffy, and he's got no hair, maybe three teeth, and the cuddly disposition of a cobra. If you walk anywhere near Sugar's car, Tuffy snarls and claws at the glass. By way of recreation, he frequently chews on Sugar's dashboard, her steering wheel more than a little too. Sugar herself is about as lively. She's a wiry, lanky woman, all sinew and veins, no fat on her at all. She wears shorts year round and shower shoes, has a wide assortment of tube tops and crepey belly shirts.

Sugar chain smokes Cools, drinks tequila, and gets pawed by men for pay while quite clearly taking no measurable interest in them.

I was out on my porch when Sugar left Ronnie's, and she shouted over to tell me, "He's pissed at you."

Then Ronnie stepped outside (dingy undershorts again) and said, "I don't know," in the way that always means he's peeved. "To hear them tell it," Ronnie went on, "I've seen the last of that truck."

We half talked it through while we waited for Sugar to get her Corolla started. She needed a new set of wires and a rotor cap, probably plugs as well, so she was usually a good ten minutes grinding before the thing took hold. If we'd had rain, it could be half an hour. Me and Ronnie took turns telling her to give it some gas or quit, and finally the engine sputtered to life like it always does, and Sugar made it nearly to the corner before she had to start it again.

Only once she was out of sight could Ronnie bring himself to inform me that my lady friend at the police department wouldn't give him his damn truck back.

"Might be because you stole it."

"Yeah, well," Ronnie said, "me and her don't see eye to eye on that."

Ronnie was thinking he could sell that truck again and probably for better money now that it had been owned briefly by a guy who'd gotten killed in a flashy way.

"People love that stuff," Ronnie told me. "Already had some nibbles."

I guessed if I was going to admire Sugar for being efficient and energetic, I'd need to throw Ronnie a little credit too. Who else would be out talking up a panel truck he didn't own that was part of an active murder investigation?

"I'm half decided I don't like that woman," Ronnie

said of Ruiz. "And what the hell's with those shoes of hers?"

I also had questions about Ruiz's shoes. I hoped she didn't have a condition and was just one of those people who didn't care what she put on her feet. In fact, I could only convince myself I had a chance at all with the woman because she didn't seem to be much interested in what she wore or how she looked. That gave me hope the man in her life wouldn't need to be so splendid. I'm guilty of thinking about that sort of thing with just about every woman I meet.

"I'll talk to her," I promised Ronnie. I needed a reason to seek out Ruiz and guessed I could tell her I was trying to do my neighbor a solid.

Then Ronnie asked me another question. "Is that Augustus on the roof?"

He pointed. I looked, and sure enough Casper and Janet's fat tabby cat was up on the front pitch over their den, licking himself alongside the chimney. I could see that the near den window was open because the curtains had blown outside.

So back over to Casper and Janet's we went, Ronnie still without any pants on. He'd gotten to where he treated the whole block like his own back hall.

"Wasn't open yesterday, was it?" he asked me.

I didn't recall and couldn't say, but once we'd mounted the porch I could see well enough that the front door wasn't shut either.

"When's the last time you were up here?"

Ronnie had to give that a think. When you're tending to a neighbor's house by doing almost nothing, it's difficult to be sure about what you might have been up to last.

"While ago," he told me eventually and then confessed, "Don't really lock it." And Ronnie held forth about the challenges of keeping up with somebody else's key.

He gave me a shove so I'd go in first. "I don't like this," he told me from back out on the porch.

I stepped into Casper and Janet's foyer. Their house wasn't anything special, a story and a half where they'd raised a couple of children and just rattled around anymore. I hadn't been inside in several years, didn't socialize with Casper and Janet, usually caught up with them when Casper was showing off improvements on their camper van.

"Looks all right, I guess," I said to Ronnie. It was just an empty entryway. The wood floor was shiny. I did notice three or four bare picture hooks on the walls.

Ronnie eased in behind me. "Where'd all the stuff go?"

"Like what?"

"You know...stuff."

Ronnie stepped into the living room, off the front

hall to the left. As I recalled, it was one of those parlors only used in calamities and full of musty empire furniture Janet's granny had bought somewhere.

"I don't like this," Ronnie said, and I saw what he meant when I joined him. Casper and Janet's living room was as empty as their front hall.

The only thing I could see fit to say at that moment was, "Glad they gave *you* the key."

There wasn't a scrap of furniture anywhere, no rugs, no pictures on the walls, no gimcrackery on the mantelpiece, no dishes in the kitchen cabinets, not even any Friskies on the linoleum anymore. It looked like somebody had come by and hauled off every stinking thing.

"You didn't see anybody?" Ronnie asked me. It sounded like an accusation.

I decided to answer him with a Bible verse. "Be sober-minded," I said. "Be watchful. Your adversary the devil prowls like a roaring lion."

Ronnie grunted and headed up the stairs in his dingy underwear.

There were two bedrooms with a bath between them in the half story upstairs, and the one on the right was as empty as the rest of the house. Then Ronnie pushed at the door to the room on the left, but it would barely swing, banged up against something solid feeling after about eight inches.

Ronnie stuck his head inside. It was all he could fit

through the gap, and he pulled back out with a funny look. "I think it's all in here."

That room was just about solid furniture, floor to ceiling and wall to wall. Full of pictures too and rolled-up rugs. I saw a toilet brush and the cat box Ronnie never scooped out. There were mattresses, nightstands, dishes and pots, even clothes from the closets, and Casper's fifty-inch TV. Everything was heaped in a pile right up to the overhead light.

"How'd they even do this?" Ronnie wanted to know. "And, you know, why and stuff?"

I'd eased my head between the jamb and the door and was trying to take it all in. "Kids maybe?" was the best I could manage.

Then I saw enough writing on the far wall to shake me up a little. Most of it was blocked by un upended settee, but I could still make out a "Ye" written in something that didn't quite look like ink.

"Uh-oh," I said to Ronnie as I was fishing out my phone. I would have been more rattled but for the chance to see Ruiz.

She didn't bring Grimes, had decided to swing by and have a look on her way home.

"Omaha?" she asked once we were up on Casper's porch, and I left Ronnie to tell her all about Casper and Janet's camper van. He described the interior fittings like a child might describe a movie, with the parts all out of order and no useful details much.

Ruiz finally went with, "Got it," by way of shutting Ronnie up. Then she stepped into the front hall, and we followed.

"The stuff's all upstairs," Ronnie told her a time or two as she toured the rooms on the ground floor and had a careful look around.

"And y'all never saw anybody over here? Didn't notice anything?"

Ronnie got a touch defensive. He had the house key after all, and while he was fine with doing nothing a responsible neighbor ought to, Ronnie didn't care for the insinuation that he'd gone the extra mile.

"Must have been like ninjas or something," he said.

Ruiz had noticed a door jamb in the den Augustus had scratched to shreds and so knew to ask me and Ronnie, "Where's the cat?"

He was still on the roof, but Augustus doesn't like to be picked up, which Ronnie discovered only once he'd climbed out an upstairs window and done it. Pretty immediately, Ronnie tossed Augustus into the shrubbery. So at the very least, the cat was off the roof.

Ronnie went searching through Casper and Janet's bathrooms for some salve. Augustus had laid into Ronnie with his back feet and taken off a layer of stomach skin.

"When did you have your last tetanus?" Ruiz asked

him.

Ronnie did a full minute of powerful math before saying, "Believe I was twelve."

Worse still, he couldn't find so much as a q-tip in either one of the medicine cabinets. It seemed like the folks who'd moved the furniture had moved every damn thing else too.

Ruiz instructed me to bull open that upstairs bedroom door, and I managed to make a gap just wide enough for us to slip through into a room where there was hardly any space for us to stand. Everything in there was piled and heaped like for a bonfire. There were canned goods from the kitchen, stuff from the freezer and liquor cupboard. A set of golf clubs and Casper's table saw. All that plus a china cupboard, a dinette table, and a tiger oak sideboard.

"Writing where?" Ruiz asked.

I led Ruiz and Ronnie in a spot of mountaineering. The words were on the far wall blocked off by a sofa set, but we all worked around to where we could see them soon enough.

I read the words out in case the fancy script was putting anybody off. "'Ye are of your father the devil, and the lusts of your father ye will do'. John, I think. Matthew maybe. One of them for sure."

Ruiz took pictures of the words with her phone, a couple of shots of the pile we'd climbed onto, and she was just about to make a call when something in the heap shifted and spooked Ronnie.

"I don't like it in here," he told us, and then something moved again, and Ronnie tried to scamper back to the door but got a leg caught under an easy-chair, and as he was attempting to work it loose, he saw something down deep in the pile.

"Y'all," Ronnie said. The tone of it turned us. "There somebody in there." He pointed.

Ruiz turned on her phone light and played it where Ronnie was pointing, down past some chair legs and below three or four loose dresser drawers. Wedged between a tin bread box and what looked like a magazine caddy, there turned out to be somebody sure enough.

He looked dead until his tongue moved. Then he found the breath to shout.

4

Anything of Casper and Janet's that fit went straight out the window and dropped into the yard. We just needed to make enough of a hole to get down to the guy and see if we couldn't maneuver him up and out.

He'd stopped yelling but would still raise whipped dog racket every now and again, and Ronnie kept telling me and Ruiz, "We ought to think on this." He'd half convinced himself the man in the pile was the old snake (Ronnie called him). "Can't know he isn't," he'd usually add, and it was tough to argue with that.

Ruiz managed to snag a couple of cops who came wailing up in cruisers and then helped us pitch more stuff into the yard. They didn't ask nearly as many questions as I would have but just acted like they'd seen all sorts of nutty doings before.

We eventually made enough of a divot for Ruiz to crawl down close to the guy and try to figure where he was stuck still and what we should shift to free him. He grabbed her arm and drew her close and moaned into her ear. Then he turned her lose so she could crawl back out.

Soon enough we got joined by Ruiz's boss, the chief or the sheriff or something. His name was Cliff and he was wearing a uniform that looked like he'd pulled it fresh from the box. His shirt and trousers both had creases where they ought to be, and in addition to a badge, he wore two showy rows of service ribbons like maybe he'd taken Berlin all by himself.

Both cops and Ruiz stopped what they were doing so they could tell him, "Sir."

He gave a head jerk and then stood there holding his hat and twirling it, and we all went back to clearing way which boss Cliff watched us at.

Eventually, he stepped over to look down into our hole and told the man at the bottom of it, "Don't you worry. We'll get you out." Then he left the room for the upstairs landing and lit what smelled like a White Owl.

The guy in the pile was half under a mattress we had a tough time moving, and he lacked the strength to pull himself clear in any useful way, but we finally did get him loose enough so he could nearly sit up. He wasn't wearing a shirt, and we shortly discovered he wasn't wearing proper trousers either but had on one of those store-bought diapers you use once you can no longer control yourself.

He looked to be about eighty, but if I'd spent a couple of days under most everything Casper and Janet had come to own, I'd probably look like I was eighty too.

He had an important thing he wanted to tell us. You could see by the way he was moving his fingers.

"Stop," Ruiz said, so we all held still. "What is it?" she asked the guy.

He said what he needed to clearly enough, and Ruiz and Ronnie looked at me in hopes that it was Biblical, but he was firing well wide of Scripture.

"Get him to say it again."

Ruiz did.

"Rene-Robert Cavelier, Sieur de La Salle." And then he said it another time, slightly louder.

After that, he sat quietly in his plastic storebought diaper until we'd worked his feet loose and finally pulled him out.

The med tech boys were on the scene by then, and Ronnie knew one of them because he'd sold the guy a scooter. That boy had bought it for his brother who kept drinking and driving and getting his license jerked, but the scooter had carburetor trouble, wouldn't even start anymore, so that fellow was convinced Ronnie owed him a repair and took that occasion to say so.

The man from the pile—Ruiz was calling him Bob—couldn't stand up without help, so Ronnie got relief when the med techs had to go and fetch their gurney, and Ruiz passed the wait trying to get Bob from the pile to talk. She asked him a string of questions about who he was and where he'd come from, and he'd nod like he was working up a pertinent response, but he ended up saying nothing at all until boss Cliff put a consoling hand on his bare shoulder when diaper guy decided to tell us, "Michilimackinac."

"What was that?" Ronnie asked me mostly. Ruiz and everybody else all looked my way as well like knowing the Bible had made me obliged to know everything else as well.

Boss Cliff had noticed the words on the wall by then. He had a dead man in his county who'd been pulverized with a brick, a guy in a diaper who couldn't yet talk sense, and weird hijinks involving a pile of household goods and a panel truck. That didn't sit well with Cliff.

"I don't like it," he said as he put on his hat. He'd let his cigar go out and pulled out a Zippo and relit it. "Don't like it at all." Cliff appeared to be speaking chiefly to Bob. Then he blew out some stinky smoke and left the room.

"He's new," Ruiz told me and Ronnie, Bob a little too.

Some of us nodded. Some of us said, "Fort Crevecoeur."

Then the med tech boys showed up with their gurney, strapped Bob down on it, and told Ronnie mostly, "Going to need some help with the stairs."

Before she left, Ruiz instructed us to put in a call to Casper and Janet, and she ran two strands of yellow police tape over their front door.

"I'm not calling them," I told Ronnie once he'd started making like he didn't know exactly how to reach Casper and Janet. Then I pointed out Augustus who was back up on the roof.

I don't sleep the way I used to. At least I don't believe I do and have gotten to where I can't remember those nights I fail to see two a.m., and I'll frequently roll out of bed and wander around. I found myself wide awake in the small hours with dead Tito on my mind along, of course, with diaper guy as well. I pulled my dad's Bible out of the box where I keep his stuff.

I'd ended up with all he had left because my sister wouldn't go near it. There was a crow he'd carved out of a block of poplar during his whittling phase and a deck of playing cards with all the Apostles on them. I'd even ended up owning the silver-plated chalice my daddy had clubbed me with along with a bright-brass cross he'd stolen (probably) from an actual sanctuary. He'd had a fair bit of Ronnie in him. His fingers were sticky all the time.

There were vestments too, including the grimy collar he used to wear, and a high-school ring from somewhere in South Carolina, along with a ballpoint pen that featured a woman dressed in a nun's habit until you turned it upside down when she went altogether nude.

All that stuff plus his King James Bible with his palm grease on the leather and his notes and markers on the tissuey pages pretty much all over the place.

Everything still smelled like him a little—Skin Bracer and tobacco with a hint of sanctimonious deceit.

At nearly four in the morning I found myself opening up his Bible and searching for those passages that were on my mind. I started with the one from Casper and Janet's, the Book of John as it turned out.

Jesus was talking on the Mount of Olives. "Ye are from beneath; I am from above, and if God were your father, ye would love me." He was being disappointed in people in his usual Jesusy way. "Ye are of your father the devil, and the lusts of your father ye will do. He was a murderer and abode not in the truth because there was no truth in him." And on it went like that, with Jesus being put out because his people were selfish and thick.

I decided to write it all down for Ruiz, print it in my tidiest hand, and I even had proper stationery for it, a high school graduation gift. It took me three or four tries to get the passage down in a way that satisfied me, and then I shifted to the Book of Revelation to work on the step van thing. That's where I met with a surprise. In my father's Bible, the passage started out with the angel down from heaven who had the key to the bottomless pit, but where I was expecting the serpent of old, I got instead "And he laid hold on the dragon, that old serpent, which is the devil," and I realized in a flash that they were using two different editions, which didn't strike me as something a murderous cult should indulge or tolerate. You'd think, at the very least, they would have agreed upon a Bible.

My father had been all in on King James. He liked the rhythm of it and the antique words while my mother was a New American Standard sort of Christian. That edition read (as far as I could tell) like it'd been written by a grumpy monk with a stick up his butt.

"Well, shit howdy," I think I told myself, "a clue."

I managed to wait until nearly half-past eight before I dialed Ruiz. We've usually slowed down at Double D's by then. Our people roll in early, likely sleep no better than I do, and just sit around in their car coats waiting for the sun to come up. I talked the matter over with Rochelle before I called her. He was a New King James man but had a brother in Georgia who'd started that way and then moved to Revised Standard, which Rochelle informed me from the griddle he considered corrupt and debased.

I could remember my father under a tent or stalking around on a stream bank with his King James Bible raised high and the verses spilling from him. It had been stirring and wondrous to hear the man, even if he was a lout, so I guessed I was original King James right with him and told Rochelle all about it until he sang four verses of "Blessed Assurance" just to shut me up.

My first call to Ruiz went to voicemail, and I wasn't ready to be concise and so ended up telling her quite a lot of nothing much at all. I called a second time to try to clean it up. I'd put some phrases together in my head, but this call she took, so I got knocked off stride again.

"Different Bibles," I kind of blurted out, a lot like Ronnie had told her, "Snapper."

There wasn't really much she could say back to me but, "What?"

So I explained it all to her, but she didn't seem to think it was much of a deal.

I had to assume she was like most people and never bothered with church but went around persuaded—like people often are—that being actively decent is kind of like faith and is probably enough.

"Are y'all at Casper's?" I asked her, was intending to set up something for later, but I guess Ruiz had other ideas because she cut me off. "Hello?"

"She's probably just busy," I told Rochelle.

He beat pancake batter and gave me "Lift High The Cross".

I couldn't make it home until half-past five because the contractor I worked for had called me in to help on a push. They had the rafters up on an addition they were building for a guy out in one of those new country subdivisions. This one was called Coventry Downs, and you either got your house with columns or got it with a mansard roof, and they were big on taupe trim paint and red front doors.

The crew needed to deck the rafters and, at the very least, run some paper because there was rain coming and the customer was raising a fuss. So I had to drive straight from Double D's and cut the half-inch plywood to whatever dimensions the boys up top called down. Then Juan hauled it up the ladder because he was agile that way and worked without pause or comment, unlike the contractor's nephew, Jason, who'd hold stuff for me that didn't need holding and otherwise stand around.

I'd trained him enough to stay out of Juan's way, but that had needed a month or two. We'd tried using him to fetch supplies, but he'd rear-ended a cement truck, had spent an hour at the Verizon store trading in his phone, and had left our lumber in the highway when he failed to strap it down. That was all on one trip, and the boss would have fired him except Jason's mother (the boss' sister) was having some kind of breakdown and needed Jason out of the house.

In a way, then, it was failed nepotism that kept me employed when the crew got slammed, because Jason couldn't seem to pick up any skills or do anything terribly useful. So the crew up top would shout down dimensions, and I'd cut the sheeting and slide it to Juan who'd hoist it onto his back and carry it up the ladder while Jason told me stuff that had popped into his head or busied himself looking at his phone.

I ended up talking to Jason that afternoon far more than I ever had before because Jason had read about dead Tito on the internet, and he couldn't help but be curious where it came to a dead guy beat with a brick and stuck in a hole.

"Weird, huh?" was how Jason boiled it down once he'd regurgitated the details, and he got as engaged as I'd ever seen him when I said I knew all about it, had even kind of met the guy.

"Truth is," I told him, "I'm working with the cops."

By then, I'd already come up with a version of the story I could tell, and I was keen to see what of it worked, even on a tool like Jason. He wasn't, I learned immediately, at all interested in the truck but owned up to a decided preference for most anything Satanic, so I quoted some Scripture at him and filled him in on the father of lies.

"What do the cops think?"

I shrugged. "A second guy turned up. This one's still alive."

"Possessed, I bet," is what Jason said.

I recalled the queer stuff diaper guy had told us and felt justified telling Jason, "A little, I guess."

Jason was reminded of another crime he'd seen on a TV show, the sort where they talk to detectives and mount cheesy recreations. A hairdresser somewhere he couldn't recall had killed a customer with poison shampoo.

"Or maybe it was her dog." Jason couldn't be sure. He tried to look it up but almost immediately got distracted by a thing he hadn't known before, a video he hadn't seen.

I arrived home to find that Casper and Janet had driven back from Omaha, and both of them were giving a lively earful to Ronnie out in the road. Janet in particular was lacing into Ronnie who she'd hoped would do next to nothing, but it turned out he hadn't even managed that. She was particularly upset about her heirlooms—she made an effort to call them—that had gotten pitched out the window and were busted up in the yard—and wasn't terribly happy somebody had smoked in her house.

Ronnie tried to squeeze in and tell her that we'd been scrambling to save a man, but that just irritated Janet all the more.

"What was he even doing in there?"

"Guess they're working on it," Ronnie said.

"And naked!"

Ronnie became a stickler. "Wearing an adult diaper."

Janet told Casper, "Give me that," and took an item from him. It turned out to be a table leg, and she hit Ronnie with it twice.

Ruiz's Ford was parked along the street, so I climbed out of my car and crossed in the vicinity of Casper and Janet and Ronnie but didn't close so far as to be in swatting range.

"He was there," Ronnie told Janet helpfully and pointed at me.

Janet gave me a curdled glance and then turned back to Ronnie who tugged up his shirt to show her what her cat had done.

"How's the van?" I asked Casper.

"Need a rethink," he said.

"Damn hard to handle in the wind."

Ruiz came out and plopped down on Casper and Janet's front steps in her paper suit.

"Bibles?" she asked me. I liked that Ruiz never troubled herself to clutter up much of anything.

"Yeah. Two different kinds."

"That matter?"

"Maybe, if you're worshipping Satan. Not if you're just throwing Scripture around."

That earned me a "Hmm."

"How's diaper guy?" I asked her.

"Seems all right. Still talking gibberish. Don't know who he is yet."

"Lot of trouble to go to," I told her. "Him and Tito both."

I'd chewed on the matter nearly all day, mostly because I was acquainted with plenty of trash and was well aware that they usually did their worst in a kind of spasm. It'd be fueled by liquor and rage, accumulated exasperation, a sense that nothing would ever get noticeably better so why the hell not go off. Our knuckleheads usually had fits at intervals instead of lives of crime.

So anybody up to something organized and dark just about had to qualify as foreign to us. That meant people who'd run across them might have noticed they were odd.

"Our freaks," I decided to tell Ruiz, "are usually all one flavor."

She looked past me, sighed, and said, "Oh, Christ." Angry Janet was heading our way.

"Is your boss here yet?" Janet asked Ruiz.

"Probably be around tomorrow, or I can give you a number for him."

Janet ignored her and looked my way. "Ronnie told me what you did." Then she snorted and stalked into her house.

Ruiz groaned and said to me, "You drink?"

5

Ruiz didn't appear to take terribly much interest in her driving, and she had a pile of stuff on the front seat and so made me ride in the back.

I decided I ought to try to chat, make an effort to be casual and breezy, but there was Plexiglass between us with quarter-sized holes drilled through it, and for the first few minutes Ruiz was talking to Grimes on her radio. She'd give him involved instructions, and he'd come back with something like, "Awright."

By the time Ruiz had finished with him and found me in the rearview, I just went with, "Where are we headed?"

"Right here."

She whipped straight across oncoming traffic, but she'd switched on her lights and siren to let people know they could stop or wish they had. We bounced over the curb cut and took two spaces in the lot of a lounge and pool hall I'd never visited before. It had been a Harley hangout for a few years when it was widely known for brawls, but then it caught fire and got rebuilt as a black roadhouse mostly, and Ruiz was nearly to the building before she remembered to come back and open my door.

They all knew her inside, and as best I could tell nobody but me was white, which left me feeling a trifle incandescent. The woman at the bar called Ruiz "Boo" and reached down a bottle of Wild Turkey while asking, without glancing my way, "Him?"

"Turkey's good," I told her and followed Ruiz to a booth in the corner.

I noticed straightaway that the placed smelled what I decided was African American. There was spice in the air, a hint of sandalwood, and something on the order of smoked goat as well. The bar lady came over with our drinks on a tray along with a bowl of ice.

"What's all this I'm hearing?" she said to Ruiz who lip farted and said back, "I know."

Then the bar lady studied me for a painful moment, a long uneasy while until Ruiz decided to introduce us but discovered that she couldn't.

"What was your name?" That stung. I'd imagined her thinking about me in detail since I'd passed some idle hours thinking about her.

I told her.

"Right. Yeah." She pointed at the bar lady. "Queenie."

"Plate of something?" Queenie asked Ruiz who nodded.

She had a sip and then another and then pulled out her ratty notebook, plucked her ballpoint from her hair.

"All right. Tell me about these Bibles."

I produced the stuff I'd written down, unfolded and flattened the pages, and started in like a man who was confident Ruiz had at least some church in her childhood because most everybody I came across did.

"Hold on," she said. "King James people?"

I explained about my father the tent revivalist and quoted a string a Proverbs at her so she could hear the music of it, which Ruiz didn't appear to do.

Queenie brought over a plate of something crispy fried and porky along with a few big chunks of cornbread and a paper towel roll.

"Didn't you ever go to church?" I asked Ruiz. She gave that question more thought than it usually rates. "A couple of funerals. One big Catholic wedding, but I was just there to arrest a bridesmaid."

"Where'd you grow up?"

"Here and there." She explained the stuff on the plate was sweet potato sticks and fried pork jowl, all of it dusted with cayenne. "You all right with that?"

I said, "Oh yeah," but I suspected I'd be parked on the toilet later. I'm not just white on the outside. I'm white down through my intestines too.

I told Ruiz what I knew about people and their choice of Bibles and slipped in plenty of personal family history, partly because it was pertinent and colorful and partly because I'd calculated it might make me seem more interesting to her, but I can't say she appeared to care.

"What am I going to get if I run you?" That was the question she finally asked me once she'd learned she was sitting across from the son of a con man and a killer.

"Set a car on fire once. Didn't really mean to. We were pretty drunk."

She waited in case there was something further, and it turned out that there was.

"Kind of stole a gas grill too, but that was mostly another kid."

"Hmm," she said. "How'd preacher daddy take it?"

"Beat me with a communion cup."

"And you still go to church?"

I shook my head. "Just got a memory for Scripture. How long have you been working around here? I don't think I've seen you before."

"Four years and a little," she told me. "I was up in Bethesda. Then Greencastle. I'd be guessing you're local."

I nodded.

"Good. Then why don't you tell me who we're looking for."

I snorted. I shrugged. "Most people in these parts don't have the energy for this. They want somebody dead, they shoot him, and if you bust in a house, you rob it. What about diaper guy?" I asked her. "Where'd he even come from?"

"Don't know yet, and he's not much help. Off in the head, I think." Ruiz checked her notebook. She'd written down some of his prattling. "Sieur de La Salle. Cataraqui, or something like it. And here's one...starved rock."

None of it meant a thing to me.

"Got him at the clinic. They're hoping his head clears up."

Ruiz pulled out a twenty dollar bill and wouldn't tolerate me quarreling about it. "Here's your job," she told me. "You get your buddy to forget about that truck."

We took a detour in the parking lot on the way to Ruiz's Ford, went up a rise just past the dumpster. Ruiz walked that way, and I followed her because I guessed she had something in mind. There was kind of a gazebo back there where people must have sat sometimes and drank, but there wasn't anybody around, just a bench and a couple of empty longnecks.

About the time I got to, "What are we...?" Ruiz turned my way and made short work of unfastening my jeans.

I was a little too stunned to say anything, but I still managed to get excited, and she peeled everything down as far as it would go and shoved me backwards onto the bench. Then she dropped the lower half of her janitorial outfit and parked herself on top of me, reached down and handled the logistics, and we proceeded to have what I would very nearly call sex.

I never kissed her. She stayed just out of reach for that, and I certainly didn't paw her but kept my hands nowhere much while she did the grinding she required and sought no assistance from me. I was her partner to the extent that I'd supplied her a piece of equipment, and she eventually grunted and climbed off, buttoned up and left for the car. I worked a splinter out of my ass, got all tucked in, and followed.

Ruiz was on the phone with somebody by the time I reached her Ford, and the back door was standing open to make it clear where I should go. She drove me back to my house about as recklessly as we'd come and didn't speak to me even once along the way.

Then she turned onto our street, stopped in the middle of the road, and I shoved my fingers through the Plexi holes hoping for some kind of communion, but all I got was a glance in the rearview as she said to me, "Get out."

I did, and off she went.

Ronnie was up on his glider, of course, since he about half lives on the thing, and he called out to ask, "Where y'all been?"

That proved convenient because it provided the perfect occasion for me to warn Ronnie off that truck.

Ronnie cackled some and told me, "Ha."

I'm guy enough to have boasted to Ronnie about

what me and Ruiz had gotten up to if I'd been able to construe it as some normal sort of thing. The trouble was I couldn't be certain exactly what had transpired between us beyond primal grinding on her end and a bit of chafing on mine. We hadn't done any of the regular stuff that usually qualifies as foreplay, and there'd been nothing remotely resembling a cuddle or even a passably cordial exchange. She took what she needed while I failed to object, and I couldn't say I'd experienced anything approaching pleasure. I could recall some pinching, some tugging, and a twinge in my lumbago, and then the prick of a splinter in my ass.

"Police going to figure this out, right?" Ronnie called to me once I was halfway across my yard.

"Yeah. Maybe. I don't know."

Then I went inside and opened a beer I'd bought because a girl was hanging out at the beer store in a t-shirt from the brewery telling us all what a grand elixir it was. The stuff tasted like it had been brewed in a brogan and then aged for a while in a stump. I swallowed a bare bit, spat out some more, and poured the rest down the sink. Then I went to bed and laid awake thinking about Ruiz until the cayenne sent me to the bathroom where I thought about her instead.

Come morning at Double D's, Rochelle was working his way through the Johnny Mathis songbook but all of it in a thundering baritone. For my part, I sponged dishes and dozed at the sink, and Becky eventually caught me at it and so poked me good before she told me, "Police."

It was Grimes, and in the little time it had taken for Becky to fetch me, he'd helped himself to a bowl of cobbler out of the carousel on the counter and appeared to be completely untoothpicked while he ate.

"She wants to bring him over," was what he told me. Even that glancing reference to Ruiz proved enough to make my splinter wound twinge.

"Bring who?"

"You know," Grimes said. I didn't. He ate. "Diaper guy."

"What for?"

Grimes had a look around. We were certainly geezer plentiful. "She figures somebody might know him."

"Fine," I told Grimes. "But he'll have, like, clothes on, right?"

"Yeah," Grimes said and then added, "My brother was with Gail for a while. Treated him about like you."

I realized at that moment I hadn't thought about Gail for a stretch. "Yeah, she's a bad one," I told Grimes and then pointed Becky's way. "You ought to run this all by her."

Grimes appeared to be acquainted with Becky to judge by the way he said, "Naw."

Then he made a phone call, got his coffee freshened,

and waited for Ruiz to roll up, which she did in a little while and then worked to get diaper guy out of the back of her car.

I got left to tell Becky who he was, or where anyway we'd found him and what Ruiz was hoping for by bringing him into the place.

"They'll need to eat," was Becky's take on stuff, which is about what I'd expected, and I told Grimes who told Ruiz, so she steered diaper guy to a table. He was wearing sky-blue surgical scrubs and looked like somebody had run a comb through his hair, and I heard him tell the fellow at the next table over something like Kankakee.

Ruiz finally got him in a chair, and he played with the napkin dispenser and the ketchup bottle and said a slew of stuff to her. I caught her eye and gave her a wave. We'd been intimate after all, but she just pointed at Grimes so I would poke him and send him over to her, and she had him go around and direct the diners' attention to diaper guy.

Nobody knew him. He sat in Double D's for most of an hour. Ruiz even fed him some hamburger steak and a pile of whipped potatoes while folks swung by to get a look up close. They were reminded, a few of them, of people, but diaper guy didn't ring any actual bells.

"Worth a try," Ruiz told me. I'd come out of the kitchen once I'd seen her paying up and heading out.

She let Grimes put diaper guy onto the back seat of her Ford, which gave me and her a sort of private moment in the lot. I figured that'd be a good chance for her to hit me with a corrective, tell me about the mistake she'd made out in that gazebo, how little it meant and why it wouldn't happen again. I was expecting that, kind of counting on it, and I was ready to throw in with her and blame the bourbon and the stress.

I'd certainly been on the receiving end of that brand of talk before because I'd gone through a phase where I'd met almost all of the women in my life at bars and lounges and roadhouses.

Sometimes the need would take hold, and we'd go at it in my car, which was not customary behavior for me or for any of the ladies, but we'd be half lit and a touch foggy on morals, which usually meant—in the ensuing days—something needed to get said. The women are almost always the ones who end up doing the talking since a guy flailing around in his car with a girl was just, you know, being a guy.

I was expecting Ruiz to go with something like, "Things got out of hand." Instead, she acted like that gazebo grinding hadn't happened at all. I got no backfilling explanation and didn't hear what a swell catch I'd be for maybe some other police lady somewhere else. She just talked to me like a witness who was helping her with a case.

"I'm wondering," she finally said to cap things off, "if you still drink."

I'd passed that motor hotel a blue million times without paying it any notice. They had a drained swimming pool and astroturf everywhere they could glue it down. It was called The Colonial in the daytime when you could make out the sign completely and The Colon in the dark because a few of the lights had burned out. It was owned by Pakistanis who also ran the gas mart up the road, and I'd never seen more than six cars in the lot.

The spot was Ruiz's choice, and she'd taken a room already by the time I got there. I'd spent a fair bit of the previous hour washing myself and sniffing my clothes, trying to settle on the proper outfit for an assignation. I wasn't sure if I should bring flowers or maybe prophylactics. Was I expected to pick up Wild Turkey or something for supper on the way? And which shoes were appropriate? I usually went with brogans, but then you're stuck unlacing the things, and what if she grew impatient with me? That seemed kind of a recipe for another splinter in my ass.

If I'd known a couple of days earlier what I'd be up to in two days' time, I would have thought we'd discovered an asteroid aiming for us. In the rational scheme of things, Ruiz and me didn't seem too likely. For one thing, she was a county cop, and I was kind of a dirtbag (if I'm honest), and while I'd been half dashing at one point in my life, time and neglect had taken the shine off most everything I'd had.

Ronnie saw me going to my car. "Where are you headed?" he asked me.

I had on my newish denim, my funeral shoes, my outlet store blazer, so I had to think there were plenty of answers Ronnie simply wouldn't buy.

"Got a date."

"Who with?"

"Girl from work. You don't know her."

"How," Ronnie wanted to know, "can you be thinking about that stuff now?"

"What stuff?"

Ronnie seemed genuinely offended. "We've got devil people around here. They'll kill you with a brick or stick you under a couple of sofas, and I hate the thought of that bunch even fooling with my truck, but you're fine taking some girl out like nothing's going on."

"What should I be doing?"

"Hell, man," he told me, "not that."

Bear in mind that Ronnie was up on his porch in his red checked bathrobe with a Milwaukee's Best in one hand and a cigarette between his lips. It wasn't like he was going to any trouble much.

"You're still seeing Sugar," I reminded him.

That raised a snort from Ronnie. "That's business,"

he said and spat. He told me, "Go on," like I was a severe disappointment to him. Then Ronnie climbed inside through a front window because his screen door tended to swell and stick.

I went to the wrong room on account of Ruiz had given me the wrong number, and I'd stopped at the drugstore on the way to pick up some protection and had bought for some reason a bag of candy corn as well. So it was me in my date ensemble with a sack from the CVS knocking on the door four spots down from the one that she came out of.

She didn't say anything, just showed herself, and then stepped back inside.

Ruiz had brought the Turkey and was drinking hers out of a plastic motel cup. The room looked about like I'd expected. One double bed. One twin. A picture over the night table of a sad clown on a tiny bicycle. A bathroom you could almost turn around in. A rack for your luggage and a shelf for everything else.

The lighting was ghastly fluorescent, and Ruiz had switched too much of it on.

"You mind?" I asked her and turned off two lamps, which Ruiz seemed to find amusing.

She hadn't come for company any more than you visit your chiropractor for a chat, and she certainly hadn't shown up for anything like romance. Ruiz behaved like a woman with a job to do, damn the surroundings and the conditions, but she seemed prepared to let me get liquored up if that's what I felt like I needed.

The question I wanted to put to her but couldn't quite swing was, "Why me?" I was afraid of what she might say back, so I let her pour me some Turkey, sat and sipped and made a bid to be sociable.

"Ever been married?" I asked her.

"Might be now," she said. "You?"

"Almost, but we thought better of it. Well, she thought better of it."

"Where is she now?"

I realized I didn't know. She'd married some other guy somewhere else. I shrugged.

Ruiz emptied her cup and refilled it. "I didn't think better of it. He's still in Pennsylvania. Likes it up there. Go figure."

"He police too?"

"Real estate." She swung around enough to favor me with her full regard. "What did you want to be?"

I didn't come from a place where picking and choosing was something you bothered with since wanting to be a thing didn't really figure into it. You ended up doing what was required. If my mother had left my father alone, I'd have been some kind of tent preacher or maybe just a greasy rowdy who helped his daddy set up and tear down.

"I don't know," I told Ruiz. "Right now I'm three

things, and even if you add them together, they don't amount to much."

She made a pouty face and whimpered to convey that I was being pathetic.

Then we had a curious kind of sex again. It was odd and exotic for me anyway and not especially enjoyable, plenty of strenuous exertion but almost all of it on Ruiz's end. I was instructed—by which I mean punched and wrangled—to limit my initiative. She had a way she liked to go at the thing, and I was made to understand I could play along with her or gather my stuff and leave.

Ruiz never came out and said anything exactly, but even I can tell when a woman's peeved and crowding disappointment. I like to think of myself as attentive when I'm having a run at a girl, but Ruiz wasn't interested in what I'll call technique and niceties. She just wanted me to lie there stiff enough to be of use. If it were possible for a man to find sex with a willing woman demeaning, I might have been on the hairy edge of that.

She talked to me some but in a curt and boot campy sort of way so I'd shift or turn or (usually) quit some quasi-tender thing I'd attempted. I was there for a task and, by God, I'd go at it precisely like she preferred.

She got what she wanted after a fairly frantic eight or ten minutes, and I could tell because I was instructed firmly not to touch her at all.

I eventually asked her about the two loops of brown

yarn on her wrist, and she looked at them like she'd never actually noticed them before. Then she bit through both, pulled them off, and handed them to me.

"You're kind of odd," I told her, which was less truth-telling than a bit of a helpless spasm.

"Can't argue with you," Ruiz said and then sat up and grabbed her shirt. She added, "Don't think I need another go."

Since she was getting dressed, I decided it would be impolite for me not to. I was pulling on my socks when I said to her, "Dinner?" only because that seemed normal. She couldn't even be bothered to snort.

Ruiz wasn't the sort to straighten a motel room before she departed from it, so I was the one who fooled with the bedspread and picked a towel up off the floor. By the time I stepped outside, she was already pulling into the road, and I didn't even think about going home but headed straight over to the pool hall where Queenie poured me a Turkey neat before I could stop her and ask for a beer instead.

"Haven't seen her," she said as she sat my drink down. "You eating?" I nodded.

"Whatever that was we had before, but a little less pepper maybe. And I just saw her."

That earned me a look from Queenie who told me, "I get all y'all through here."

I wasn't anxious to find out how large a club I'd joined

in allowing myself to be made use of by Ruiz, partly because I had a jealous streak and partly because my prophylactics were all still in the box and it was sealed.

"She's a tough nut," is what I went with.

Queenie giggled.

"Good cop, I guess."

"Don't know about that, but your sort sure seems to like her."

"What's my sort exactly?" I regretted it immediately out of fear that Queenie might tell me. Fortunately, a guy came in and sat down the bar, so she went to him instead.

I recognized him from Double D's. Two eggs poached, oatmeal, and bacon. He was a large man with a fuzzy white beard he'd thought way too much about. It had edges and angles in curious places, and they were stark against his skin because he was about the color of tire rubber.

"You lost?" He was looking towards the bar back, but I knew he was talking to me.

"Maybe. A little," I told him.

"Girl trouble," Queenie said.

"I had some of that once," oatmeal man announced. "Way back."

He laughed. She laughed. I smiled, and that's about when Rochelle came in. He briefly squinted my way as he kissed oatmeal man on the lips. Queenie started in on a cocktail for him with fruit juices and weird liquors.

Rochelle and his buddy did the neighborly thing and slid down the bar my way.

I switched to beer, ate a lot of fried something, and took part in the brand of cultural exchange that probably ought to be required of every white guy around. I was outnumbered and confused about half the time, mostly because I was lingo-deficient, but I managed to get acclimated and clued in after a bit.

Rochelle tried to tell me his friend's name was Cody, but I insisted Cody was only a name that white weather women gave their blonde babies until Rochelle's Cody explained his folks had spelled his with an ie and a q.

"I cleaned it up," he told me and then described his parents who proved to be the black variation of your basic hippie mom and dad. Instead of free love and hash, Cody's folks were all in on tribal, sub-Saharan stuff.

"I feel about a dashiki," Cody told me, "the way you do about a jello mold."

So we weren't all that different once I'd calibrated for perspective, and it didn't take long for me to not care that everybody who walked in was black.

"He's one of Ed's," Queenie eventually informed Cody and Rochelle.

Rochelle kind of knew already from scraps and bits I'd said in the kitchen, but I'd not been aware that people generally were acquainted with Ruiz's rep.

"Remember that boy with all the hardware?" Queenie pointed at her ear. She was talking exclusively to Rochelle and Cody.

"Never been past Culpeper? That one?" Rochelle asked.

Queenie nodded and then turned my way and listed all of that boy's offenses against proper public behavior, against grooming, against dignity. "He sat right where you are and cried. She'd just gone off. He couldn't find her, and I don't even think he had a load on, and him all inked from his armpits down."

"I don't feel teary," I told them all. "Just, you know, a little confused."

"Had a few of them too," Queenie allowed, but before she and Rochelle and Cody could give me chapter and verse on other assorted menfriends of Ruiz, I went ahead and owned up to not wanting to hear about them.

I moved onto carnage just to change the subject. I was more comfortable, I have to confess, with a guy tenderized by a brick than a woman treating me like a utensil.

"You heard all about this, didn't you?" I asked them. "Dead man in a hole? Live one under a pile of sofas and stuff?"

And they had heard about it but only the way we usually hear about things, which is scattershot and incomplete and ordinarily half wrong. We don't have a central reliable source for local information beyond Craigslist if you're hoping to buy a cord of seasoned firewood. For police matters, there's the online blotter, but that's mostly people getting caught driving drunk, which we would have found out about anyway once we'd seen them on a scooter.

"I heard they cut him," Cody told me.

"Who? Which?" Queenie asked.

"One in the hole."

"Naw," I told Cody. "They beat him with a brick."

"How about the sofa guy?" he asked me.

"I'm not sure they did anything to him. He was only wearing a diaper and had gotten left to smother, I guess."

"I saw him," Rochelle told Cody and Queenie. "Looked like somebody's grandpa."

"He from around here?" Queenie asked me.

"Don't know. He's not in his proper mind, and I don't think he remembers how he ended up where he was. Ruiz hasn't told you about this?" I asked Queenie.

"We're not friendly like that," she said.

And it went that way for close to an hour before we ran out of chat and I paid up and went home. I was pleased with myself for having some new acquaintances since I'd lately noticed I was one of those guys who no longer had what I'd call friends. I had workmates and neighbors, people I saw repeatedly but who only knew about me that I showed up for a job or lived in a house up the street. Ronnie was aware I had a car and would drive him places in it, while Janet and Casper had decided that, out of all their immediate neighbors, I was the one who wouldn't get a key.

I was on good terms with the hoarder at the corner who drove one of those boxy Korean wagons she'd filled with magazines and items of clothing except for the hollow where she sat.

A plumber had been in her house once and had come out flummoxed and shaken. When we tried to explain our neighbor Kay was widely known to be kind of a pack rat, he told us, "I'm kind of a pack rat. That woman there's a nut."

He wasn't wrong, but she was our nut, so we made allowances for Kay just like we made them for Ronnie who occasionally slipped up and plundered stuff from neighbors' yards. And there was a couple down the street whose daughter had gone off and stuck them with her children who were wild and mean and ferociously destructive and didn't mind their grandparents at all. Some one of us would occasionally give those kids a smack since their grandma and grandpa were a little too lax and infirm to do it themselves. We did kind of the same thing with the bird dog at the junction who woke up each morning convinced he'd never seen a squirrel before.

That was my crew, my tribe, and we looked after each other, frequently without making mention of it or even letting on. There were people on our road I wouldn't see for many weeks, but I'd notice if their lights went on and their cars drove in and out. It might be neighborliness of the barest sort, but in this world it's still a bond, which is why Ronnie had talked about getting the street together for a chat.

"There's riff-raff around," was how he put it. "Need to let them all know it."

He was sincere about that and unironic since Ronnie might have been a thief and a rascal, but he almost always succeeded at being them somewhere else. He didn't want Satanic trash anywhere on our street, and Ronnie proposed that just about everybody would probably share that view.

We did have a couple of neighbors who seemed down on decency. Gunther had been in the hauling business, but he'd retired from that, and his wife had endured him idle at home for close to half a year before she went to visit her sister in Burlington and couldn't be tempted back. Gunther went from grumpy to cantankerous, flew the stars and bars off his porch and had a shotgun ready for anybody who dared step in his yard. That meant the meter reader and the postman and the girl scouts and the Mormons and most especially the guys who delivered the phonebooks because they were usually Mexican or black.

Gunther stayed filthy and was unsavory, a legitimate

abomination, but when the deputies would get called in and come through to ask us about him, we'd say he was eccentric and more than a little misunderstood because he was our neighbor and lived just up the street. That went as well for the lady from Rhode Island who we looked out for too even though she talked a mile a minute with some daft Yankee accent, and we couldn't understand a word she said.

While I knew Ronnie was keen to organize a neighborhood meeting, I'd also had long exposure to Ronnie's lack of follow through, so I was certainly surprised when I came rolling home from my night out at The Colon and the pool hall and there was a neighborhood quorum listening to Ronnie in the middle of the road. It looked like everybody, even cantankerous Gunther and the lady from Rhode Island who'd brought her night sitter with her to put into Woonsocket English whatever Ronnie said.

Once I'd walked over, I got pressed to explain why I was wearing a blazer and looking spiffy, but Ronnie took the lead on filling them all in. He said where I'd been and what I'd been up to and made it clear that, while he was a hound himself, there were limits to what he'd do.

"Bigger fish, dammit," was how Ronnie chose to put it. "And I been asking around," he told me. "Ain't no girls from work."

"Alright, fine," I said to Ronnie and the rest of them.

"I was meeting with that lady cop, thought maybe she'd tell me more if we were out and, you know, friendly."

Then they wanted to hear if I'd taken her to dinner and where exactly and what both of us had, so I was obliged to spin a story and make up a couple of entrees you might could get at Lorenzo's if you were willing to drive a half hour for red sauce and the sort of chianti you could strip varnish with.

"Did she wear those shoes?" Ronnie wanted to know.

"Different, but still a lot like them."

"Must be a foot thing."

By then our Rhode Island neighbor's sitter was translating and explaining in overtime.

"What about us?" Casper asked me once Janet had elbowed him twice. "Y'all busted our stuff. I know they made you, but those two china cabinets that went out the window...her granddaddy built them both." Casper glanced Janet's way and she looked appropriately miffed and sad.

Ronnie made the case for the two of us being victims just like them. That prompted Janet to mention the stolen truck Ronnie had parked in their driveway, which got Kay going because of all the stuff you could put inside a vehicle like that.

The couple with the grandkids kept taking turns leaving to go check on their house since there was a better than even chance their grandchildren were wrecking the place.

"They think it's kids, with the brick and all?" somebody asked me. It turned out to be a guy in a pajama
top I didn't know. Ronnie introduced him as Kay's little
brother who was staying in her carport for a while.

"Didn't get that feeling," I told him.

"I had a wild phase when I was, like, sixteen," he said.
"We'd get stirred up and do crazy mess sometimes."

"Don't listen to him," Kay told us. "He's had one
phase, and this is it."

Janet elbowed Casper who put us back on point.
"What's she saying, that lady cop?"

"Still waiting on lab work," I told him. "Don't think
they've identified the guy from your house, and I didn't
get the feeling they have too much on that dead sheetrocker yet.

Gunther the cranky hauler announced he'd once
been arrested by that Mexican girl for firing his shotgun at some fools.

"I was drunk," he explained. "She was all right but
put the cuffs on too damn tight."

"They say they might get fingerprints or something,"
I told everybody, "in the next day or three."

"Why don't y'all poke around," Casper chimed in.
"You two," he added and pointed at me and Ronnie with
his nose.

When the two of us failed to display any measurable

enthusiasm for that idea, Janet informed all our neighbors, "They're the cause of this, don't you know." Then she told where that step van had come from and who had carried Ronnie to it.

"Guess it wouldn't hurt to stir the pot," Ronnie declared. "Like Sherlock," he added, "and you know, Simpson. Start in the morning, won't we?"

"Got to work," I told him.

"Then here's what we'll do." Ronnie scrunched up his face like he was calculating. "We'll start in the afternoon."

6

Ruiz's Ford was parked at Casper and Janet's by the time I got off at Double D's, and Grimes was leaning against the front grill talking to somebody on his phone. Ruiz was inside getting guff from Janet, so I waited out in the porch where I could hear their conversation well enough. It sounded like Ruiz and them had finally put a name to diaper guy—Charles Erskine Everall from down around Petersburg. He'd been a history professor over at Hampden Sydney for a while.

Janet kept saying, "We don't know the man" as Ruiz gave Janet his details. Mr. Everall was missing from some assisted-living spot, and he had a daughter in Germany who'd decided to stay put because they were on the outs.

"How'd he get in here?" Janet wanted to know.

Ruiz must have shrugged because Janet had one of her snippy fits. I'd been the target of a few of those myself. When Janet expects one thing from you but you and give her another, she goes huffy and snorty and sour, and she did all of that to Ruiz.

"How does knowing his name make any difference?"

she finally found the words to ask.

Ruiz started in on the case for tracking down Charles Erskine Everall's recent movements, but Janet interrupted by fairly shouting, "To me?"

Then I heard more talk about Janet's china cupboards, and it sounded like she had become considerably fonder of a cedar wardrobe since it had gone out the window and busted into four pieces on the ground.

Ruiz probably could have gotten a bit of mileage out of even the feeblest apology. All she had to do was regret how stuff had been spoiled and broken in the pursuit of saving a man from probably certain death. But either Ruiz wasn't built to apologize or Janet had triggered her somehow, so one of them moaned and sputtered while the other did nothing at all.

The best Janet could get from Ruiz was instructions to call her insurance agent. "Give him your details," Ruiz said, "and we'll confirm."

Then Ruiz endured a brief description of Janet's sainted dead grandfather, or most of a description anyway. Ruiz showed up at the door screen while the man was still fighting in France, and when Janet spied me on her front porch, she clammed up and retreated, so Ruiz seemed nearly grateful by the time she came outside.

"What's up?" she asked me but with less vinegar than normal.

"The neighbors all got together," I told her. "We're

hoping you can meet with us and maybe fill us in."

"Can't."

"Anything'll do."

"You tell them."

"Ought to come from you."

She scratched like a man might and checked the sky. "This about last night?"

"No." And it wasn't, not even slightly. "People here are nervous, and nobody's telling us much."

"Lab's slow. Beyond this Everall, we've got nothing cooking yet."

"Fine. Come around and say that."

She scratched some more, and finally told me, more or less, "Naw."

Then she was off the porch and halfway to her Ford when Ronnie came out of his house in a suit I'd never seen before. It was green and not a pleasant shade, more like outlet clearance lime.

"She any help?" he asked while eyeing Ruiz's Grand Marquis. Once I shook my head, Ronnie said, "That means you and me, I guess."

"Doing what?"

"Scene of the crime," he told me. "Got my Sherlocking outfit on."

I stopped for gas at a Kangaroo Mart, and Ronnie bought a tube of barbecued Pringles that he shared with me on the way out to Whelan country and that farm.

"A fingerprint'll probably break it." I told Ronnie as we went. That was my general line on the thing because it let me out of working up any sort of elaborate theory about why people would traffic in Bible verses as well as death by brick.

As a grown-up, I'd come around to the view that humans are disappointing and will almost always do what they want instead of what they should. There were sure to be exceptions, of course, the kind of thoughtful, selfless people who we all stumble onto every now and again, but more and more that's a bit like running across a pterodactyl. You could, but you probably won't, and once you have, you'll wish you hadn't because people who do the right thing can be damn hard to tolerate.

I was personally kind of in the middle, what I'll call situationally decent, while Ronnie was ninety percent shifty lies and grease. He had a few lines he wouldn't cross and stuff he wouldn't do, but he never quite knew where a line like that was until he was standing on it.

Consequently, bringing dastardly people to justice hadn't struck me as an activity Ronnie would have much interest in, so I kept waiting for him to confess to me what we were actually about. Instead, he ate Pringles and wiped his greasy hands on my upholstery while airing random thoughts that bubbled up into his head.

"Kept thinking I'd be taller," Ronnie said. And then after about five minutes, "Lost my belt somewhere.

How do you even do that?" He ate more Pringles, read the tube. "Tell me these aren't made with that stuff that gives you the runs."

All I had to do was drive and shrug and wait for Ronnie to run out of palaver so I could finally ask him, "What have you got in mind for us?"

"I figure there's something out here at this place that's drawing these devil people, and me and you and Buck here ought to find out what it is."

Buck was the name Ronnie had given his pistol, and he reached around and pulled it out of his pants. I'd seen Buck plenty of times before. He was a snub-nosed .38. Ronnie kept Buck in a sock on his nightstand and would bring him out for display those occasions when there was rowdiness on the street.

For a thieving rascal, Ronnie was awfully particular about his shut-eye and insisted he needed a good seven hours at least five nights a week, which made noise out on the road something Ronnie wouldn't stand for. So out Buck would come, and Ronnie would switch on his porchlight and step outside, quite frequently in the al-together, and he'd tell whoever needed to hear it, "Shut up!"

Every now and then, Ronnie would fire a shot (more than once into his porch ceiling), so by the time he'd driven the trouble away, the whole damn road was awake.

"Got bullets left?" is what I asked him because Ronnie was exactly the sort of guy who'd only regret not having bullets once he'd met with a dozen devil people to shoot.

"Oh yeah," Ronnie told me, and he dropped the cylinder and showed me two whole rounds. I made him dump them in his hand so I could be sure they weren't just a couple of casings. You never quite knew with Ronnie because he didn't focus on details much.

"Where's yours?" he asked me.

I had the Colt Peacemaker my mother had killed my father with, which had originally belonged to her grandfather. Since it was antique and pricey to shoot and had kind of a troubled history, I didn't get the thing out and fire it all that that much. It stayed loaded and wrapped in a towel down in the bottom drawer of my dresser under the trousers I couldn't convince myself I'd never squeeze into again.

"Back home," I told Ronnie. "If we find anybody, I'm calling Ruiz and them."

"Won't need them," Ronnie said. "It's going to be fools from money because that's how it always is." Ronnie ticked off examples. He had four of them altogether, but three of them came from movies it didn't sound like Ronnie had seen. Only one was real and authentic, but it did speak to Ronnie's point.

There'd been a bunch out west in the mountains,

stuck back in some crease of the Alleghenies, who'd organized and gathered around yoga and meditation but branched off into illicit narcotics soon enough. Pharmaceuticals chiefly but some heroin as well, and that crew became notorious for their sheer ruthlessness, not what you'd expect from transcendental pigeon posers.

People who stole from them or failed to pay them or just annoyed them in some way would get warned once and then made examples of—as in tortured and killed in some colorful fashion and displayed occasionally on a pike. That crew also made excellent carrot cake that they sold to the Mennonites.

"Whatever happened to them?" I asked Ronnie.

"That's what I'm saying. Their daddies or somebody hired lawyers, the real kind from up in NOVA. Half of them are out already, and the bad ones got maybe eight to ten."

"So this bunch comes from money too?"

Ronnie looked pleased I was catching on. "We tell them we can run them in or they can buy us off, and then, you know, we just negotiate."

"Could be they'll beat us with a brick."

Ronnie allowed he'd thought of that and showed me one more time his stubby pistol.

"Let's hope there are only two of them," I said.

That farm felt quite a lot creepier this time through even if it looked the same. I parked up at the pipe gate, and we walked down the weathered track, past the cow lot choked with saplings to the first barn with the roof caved in.

The smell was all snake and stale livestock dander along with that night soil stink you get once manure has gone to dirt. There was what looked like a half-licked mineral block sitting in a rotted trough and some empty fertilizer bags and a disassembled bush hog. Nobody had written in blood or piled up household goods in a provocative way. I gave Ronnie all the time he wanted to figure that out for himself.

Next we went to the farmhouse, but the floors in there were rotten, so once Ronnie suggested I go upstairs and have maybe a quick look around, I told him, "Naw," and we just kept on going.

The other big barn was about the same—nothing but farm stink and rotted timbers—and then we moved on to the last standing structure, a shed out past an old frost-blasted slab of cement where a pig parlor or something used to be.

There was a workbench inside with coffee cans on it and a chainsaw with its guts laid out. That stuff was all dusty and looked like it had been sitting around for a decade, but we could see on the floor that the layer of grit had been walked through and disturbed since then.

"Did Grimes come in here?" Ronnie asked me.

I remembered it was all Ruiz could do to get him to

stick his head in the house. "Don't believe so," I said, "but with all those cops at the pond, some other one might have."

That probably would have satisfied Ronnie, and it seemed reasonable enough to me, but then he went and found an item stuck in the vice at the far end of the workbench. It was the sort of babydoll any normal person would probably have nightmares about. The thing looked to have had yellow yarn hair once, but somebody had cut it off, and it probably had clothes, but they'd been removed, so the thing was all white muslin and stitching.

The features on the face were made from black thread—a mouth, a nose in profile, two eyes that came off looking in slightly different directions. And on the plump front torso (it was a soft doll, full of stuffing) somebody had drawn a heart about where one would be. It wasn't, however, a valentine heart but was instead a decent version of the actual human kind, a muscle with veins across it and arteries poking out of the top.

Ronnie dropped the thing pretty immediately, pushed past me, and went outside. I picked it up and followed him. "You all right?"

He was drawing deep breaths as he leaned over and held his knees. "Lord I hate a doll," he said.

"Is kind of a creeper," I told him. "Can't have been here long." I sniffed the thing. "Smells flowery, like soap or something."

"My grandma had a room full of dolls," Ronnie informed me. "She used to put me in there whenever I acted up. One of them had these big black eyes, and if you moved her at all, she squeaked."

I did the math on whether a room full of dolls was worse than a beating with a chalice, and Ronnie kept coming out on the short end of the thing.

"You see the heart?" I asked him.

I tried to hand that doll to Ronnie, but he refused to take it. "Didn't I just say I had a thing?"

"Even out here?" The sky was blue. The sun was shining. And Ronnie's grandma was surely dead with her dolls scattered to the wind.

"Yeah, out here." He said it emphatically enough to make me understand that he was damaged and scarred and wasn't playing at being afraid like he played at most everything else.

I think I said, "Oh," and then wondered if maybe we ought to call Grimes and Ruiz, but my Sherlock said, "Uh-uh," and then appeared to vomit just a little.

We visited the pecan grove again and stood where we'd stood before. Ronnie picked up a weathered cigarette butt and examined it with interest before he tossed it aside and plucked up another for a bit of close study as well.

"Cops maybe," I suggested.

"Or devil people. Hell," Ronnie said, "they might as well smoke."

We walked across the pasture in the direction of the pond where dead Tito had been stuck in a hole on the bank. We got as far as the crest of the rise and stopped there, decided we could see all we needed from up top.

"Who found him?" Ronnie asked me. "Who'd even be coming out here?"

That was a useful question that I'd not thought to ask, so I pulled out my phone and called Ruiz, told her voicemail what I wanted. After a couple of minutes, she texted back. Her message said, "Some girl."

"Out here?" Ronnie asked me. "What girl? Where from?

So it seemed that Ronnie could, in fact, Sherlock at least a little. He wasn't steady with a theory, but he knew what he wanted to know.

We both opened maps up on our phones to find out what the surrounding territory looked like. We could see where we were and where we'd come from, but there was nothing much past that pond, just some woods and a hedgerow and then another farm.

Ronnie pointed out a path something had made up through the pasture above us towards the treeline.

"As long as we're here," he told me.

That wasn't at all a Ronnie thing since he wasn't given to economizing and never took care of business just because he was handy for it. I caught myself thinking of Ronnie as two distinctly different creatures. There was front-porch Ronnie who laid around wondering what exactly he ought to steal next and Sherlock Ronnie who could take his mysteries one detail at a time.

It occurred to me that wasn't far off from my pair of personas. I was a schlub with a cheating ex-girlfriend and a trio of lousy of jobs and yet also a man with a cop sex buddy and an encyclopedic knowledge of Scripture.

I kind of felt about the deep woods the way that Ronnie felt about dolls. I may have never had a grandma who used to toss me into the forest, but I got lost once with a neighbor's dog and chased by a bear into a thicket, and the whole ordeal stuck with me and shook me up.

My mother had asked our neighbor to watch me while she carried my sister somewhere, but it was one of those deals where I was expected to amuse myself and stay put because the neighbor I'd been left with liked her gin a lot, and by midday she'd was usually unfit for watching much of anything.

That woman had a collie name Hobart. This was back in the day when people often owned collies or dachshunds, occasionally dalmatians, and you could have toured the county and not seen a labrador once. Hobart would nip your ankles when you ran, and his coat would get tangled and matted, so our rummy neighbor would trim him up with her pinking shears, and he'd come out looking about like you'd expect. Gappy, pitted, a bit scraped and bloodied except up around his head where he'd usually get left alone.

Hobart had recently gotten one of his trims, so you could see his ticks all over, and I was pulling them off and burning them because I was at that age when the sight of fire and the stink of matchbook sulfur were all but hypnotic to me. That dog, however, was well short of enthralled and tried to escape into the woods.

We had a stretch of forest off our back lot that gave onto a run of high tension lines and, beyond them, more forest, probably a couple of hundred acres. Prior to that day, the woods were just like everything else for me, so I didn't hesitate to follow Hobart at a trot. Soon enough we were back past the power lines, and it was all I could do to keep Hobart in sight.

Then I heard him yelp in an uncommon way and looked up to find him coming towards me at a gallop. He shot past me and kept on going, and the bear that was chasing him arrived. I'd never seen a bear up close like that. I'd certainly never smelled one. The claws and the teeth right there within reach were terrible enough, but the musky stink of that creature was more powerful and wild than I would have imagined.

I backed up between a pair of trees, each of them no bigger around than a drain pipe, and that bear chuffed at me and stuck a paw between them for a swipe. Then her cub, I guess, let out a cry back over where she'd come from, and she gave me a final snort and headed off.

Hobart must have been lurking because he was right up on me in a flash, all bright-eyed and panting and wholly delighted with the mischief he'd stirred up. Before that, I'd only ever thought of the woods as a shady place where you could get away from the flies when they were biting and find toadstools and moss and frogs if you knew where to look. The only bears I'd ever seen had always run the other way, but then I'd gone and chased Hobart straight into a different sort of thing.

While I never told anybody about any of it, I became the kid who, given the choice, would always stay in the yard.

So I followed Ronnie across the pasture and right up to the treeline, which started with scrubby slash pines and sugar maples and then went to sapling oaks and bigger stuff. I slowed down and finally stopped about the time I'd reached the poplars while Ronnie kept going and kept on talking like I was hard behind him all the while.

He finally noticed I'd dropped off and came back to where I was standing. "What?" he said.

I thought maybe in the spirit of the working partnership of Sherlock and Simpson I ought to share with Ronnie a full explanation of why I was stuck where I was, especially since he'd told me all about his grandma and her dolls.

Instead I decided to go with, "I don't like the woods."

"Come on," he told me and headed back in, but I stayed right where I'd planted.

"I'm not kidding. I can't go in there."

He didn't respond like a grown man afraid of baby dolls ought to, which I pointed out to him after he'd told me what a fool I was.

"That's different," was all he could manage, even once I'd explained how it wasn't, so we were having a bit of a pitched exchange out there in the ratty scrub when what turned out to be a hickory nut passed between us.

"You see that?" I asked Ronnie.

"Saw something."

I looked around for a hickory tree and maybe an irate squirrel but saw nothing that would qualify as either. And I was about to let it go and take up my case again when another hickory nut came flying out and hit Ronnie in the side of the head.

"Hey!" he yelled at the forest generally and, of course, fished out his pistol.

"Might just be a squirrel," I told him because I knew he was trigger happy. I'd seen Ronnie fire Buck from his porch at cats and stuff, not that he was the sort who could ever hope to hit the thing he aimed at, but he did once bounce a slug off the road and put it in Casper' camper van.

"Somebody's in there." Ronnie took a couple of steps towards the treeline.

And he'd just about finished talking when two nuts together found us. One of them hit me in the shoulder, and that was all Ronnie required. "All right," he said and charged towards the tree line. He'd raised Buck and fired off his only two bullets when the rest of the stuff started coming out.

More hickory nuts but some pine knots too and what looked like spears made from saplings and branches along with a fair number of plain old rocks. How Ronnie failed to get skewered I'll never know, but he sure got dinged a time or two, enough to turn him around and send him charging past me.

I'd soon joined Ronnie in what would prove our leading Sherlock and Simpson maneuver. We retreated from that tree line at a run.

7

I've long since made my peace with the fact that I'm not brave and noble, and I've found a way to be satisfied with plodding and reliable instead, but even still I wonder sometimes how it might feel to have more pluck. I'm not convinced I'd be extravagantly better for it, but I'd probably find myself on a different path than the one I've long been on, which had me following Ronnie down past the barns and beyond the mildewed farmhouse.

"Got hickory nuts in the Bible?" he wanted to know.

"Don't think so."

"Look," Ronnie said and pointed. Up on the hilltop where we'd been, something was fixed to one of the trees. It was up in the limbs and flapping. A square of cloth the size of a bedspread, and it was white mostly with stray patches of dark.

"We ought to go back up there," Ronnie told me, but I knew he didn't mean it. He sometimes likes to make a show of being eager and impetuous, of being the kind of unbridled man who needs to get held back.

"Buck's empty," I reminded him.

That was all the restraining Ronnie required.

We waited at the pipe gate once I'd turned my car around on the outside chance that whoever had been in the woods would come down and swarm up on us. On the phone with Ruiz, I'd made it all sound as evil and pressing as I could.

She sure didn't hurry because me and Ronnie had the leisure to pass through several stages of apprehension from fully expecting to be safe because we were hanging near my car to wondering if maybe the crew from the woods had barricaded the road ahead and we'd find them waiting on us, each with maybe a paver in hand.

So we were edgy and nervous but not in a ready-for-any-damn-thing kind of way. More like bottled-up frantic and so agitated that all we could do was pace and smoke. I quit cigarettes some years ago, but I bummed a couple from Ronnie even though he'd lately switched to some cheap-ass menthols that tasted like a Christmas wreath on fire.

When I complained, Ronnie went off for a stretch on federal agricultural policy where it pertained specifically to tobacco yields, a topic he clearly knew slightly less than nothing about. It did serve as a useful distraction for us and a chance for Ronnie to be down on the federal government, which he was at some length for a guy who'd never voted even once.

Eventually, Ruiz showed up alone in her Grand Marquis, and Ronnie got on her straightway for having failed to call in SWAT.

"They don't do hickory nuts," she told him, which Ronnie lurched around and sputtered about. "What are you even wearing?"

It got left to me to tell her, "That's Ronnie's Sherlocking suit."

"Show her," Ronnie instructed me, so I walked Ruiz far enough down the track to where we could get a clear view up to the treeline. The breeze had died, and that big square of cloth was hanging limp by then, which made it look more like litter than intimidation.

"Well," Ruiz said, "let's go see."

Ronnie lobbied her for bullets, but when she asked to see his gun and he pulled it out and handed it to her, she threw it deep into the cow lot, and it sank into the weeds.

Ronnie stayed mad and wouldn't talk clear up to the pecan grove where he finally thawed enough to say, "We found a baby doll."

"A what?"

"You know." Ronnie described an item with his hands that could have been a butternut squash.

"Had a heart on it. The real kind."

It fell to me to explain everything Ronnie meant.

"Find out who owns this place yet?" I asked.

Ruiz pulled out her notebook and read off a name.

Some Galloway, as it turned out, when I'd been expecting a Whelan, if even one by marriage or twice removed.

"Know any Galloways?" I asked Ronnie.

"Naw," he said and left it at that, but Ronnie confessed to me later he'd stolen a Gator—one of those beefed up golf carts—from a Galloway living out on the landfill road.

"He didn't have no land. Didn't need that thing. It was just sitting in his yard."

Ruiz charged right up the hillside—her ugly shoes seemed good for that—while we came along behind her with less zip and energy. She didn't even have her gun out or a nightstick or anything but simply closed on that treeline empty-handed and finally stopped at the scrubby border to see just what manner of item was hanging there.

I don't know if she recognized what it was, but I sure did straightaway because I'd done my share of drywall work and more than a little painting and still owned a couple of drop cloths like the one attached to that tree. One corner was tied to a branch with the rest left free to droop or blow.

"Got to be Tito's," I told them both and pointed out a couple of conspicuous spots of what looked like dried joint compound.

The thing was attached too high to reach from the ground, so Ruiz glanced my way and said, "Get it."

Ronnie wouldn't let me. He stopped me with a nudge and went over and started climbing after he'd paused to tell Ruiz that it turned out I was kind of scared of trees.

I kept waiting for a hickory nut or something worse to come flying at us out of the forest, maybe a flaming pine knot or a bucket of molten tar, but Ruiz hardly paid any attention at all to the stretch of woods before us because she had a drop cloth to inspect and she was a one-thing-at-a-time sort of girl.

"Why drag it up here?" Ronnie asked once he'd untied the thing and dropped it to the ground.

Ruiz shook her head, couldn't really say, and finally pulled out her sidearm. She dropped her clip to check it, and I was pleased to see it filled with all the bullets it could hold.

"Stay behind me," was the instruction we got as Ruiz stepped towards the treeline, and that felt like something we could probably do pretty well. Especially me, since I was half tempted to wait for them to come back out, but I had to think it'd be just like minions of Satan to set upon me while I was lingering in the thickety scrub alone.

So into the forest the three of us went, and I worked to choke back my anxiety once the canopy had thickened overhead and the light had gone half dim. It was oaks mostly with some poplars mixed in, all of them towering and mature and no underbrush except for moss and the occasional clump of toadstools, so you could see for a stretch but not well or clearly because the light was low.

"What's that over there?" Ruiz asked.

I was dividing my time between looking for violent, misguided souls and bears. Snakes too, of course, but just about every stick on the ground could pass. Let's just say I wasn't at my ease even before we'd reached that pile of rocks. All basalt and quartz—the local stuff—and piled about six feet high. Actually, it was more of a stack and looked to be around two feet across at the bottom.

"Is this something people around here do?" Ruiz wanted to know.

"Is now, I guess," Ronnie told her.

"There's a thing stuck in there." I pointed out a piece of something that looked metallic and was wedged between a couple of rocks maybe five feet up.

I couldn't help but notice that Ruiz wasn't awfully particular with it, didn't bother with gloves or her ballpoint or anything but just scrabbled around with her bare fingers until she could fish the thing out. It was a wristwatch, an old Hamilton with the crystal cracked and only one leg of the band, the side without the buckle. The hands had stopped at 8:14.

"You don't figure somebody's in there, do you?" That seemed like a reasonable question from Ronnie given how what was reasonable had shifted from where we used to think it was.

Ruiz shook her head and shrugged.

"SWAT, yeah?" When Ronnie had a thing on his mind, it often stayed there for a while.

Ruiz dropped and checked her clip again. "Let's see what else is in here," and off she went.

It wasn't like we were about to hang by a pile of rocks with a guy maybe in it, so me and Ronnie followed Ruiz deeper into the woods.

Ronnie talked all the while. It was a nervous thing with him. I'll go quiet when I'm worked up, but Ronnie always talks and not about anything pertinent. This time he got off on fencing somehow and spoke at length about the hot wires people string around horses and cows. Ronnie claimed to know a boy who fell into one once, and it caught his shirt on fire.

"Do something with him," Ruiz told me after a while.

I said back to her, "You've got the gun."

Ronnie recouped some credit when he saw a thing in a tree, an item bound together with strips of bark and made out of sticks and feathers. It wasn't shaped like anything much but was just a confusion of stuff attached together, including a yellow hair ribbon, which is what had caught Ronnie's eye.

Ruiz just needed to glance at Ronnie to send him scampering up the trunk, and once he'd moved that thing off the spot where it was resting, he uncovered a strip of paper.

"More Bible stuff," he said.

So I got to be something other than merely nervous. Ronnie floated the scrap of paper down.

"Everyone who does evil," was written on it, "hates the light."

"Book of John," I told Ruiz.

"SWAT now?" Ronnie tossed that twig and hair ribbon thing down where I could catch it.

Ruiz found more rocks in a shorter pile and then a ring of them around a fire hole. In its way, it was all worse than running across even a couple of bears.

"Where are we even going?" Ronnie asked Ruiz after a while, and he did it so frequently and in such a pitiful whine that I don't how she didn't mace him.

We came come across the pelt of a raccoon spiked, head down, to the trunk of a tree and also one of those spring-loaded pie pans you used to block up stovepipes with. They often came painted and decorated. This one had a silo on it, and that's where we decided to stop and quit.

Ruiz still didn't call SWAT but made do with Grimes and them. The pair from the panel truck—Flynn and the chirpy girl—came straggling up with a couple of colleagues, and those four started being particular all over the damn place.

First, they collected the drop cloth and photographed

and bagged it. Then they shifted to the stack of rocks and had quite a confab about it. Flynn and his chirpy partner decided to take the stack down once they'd taken pictures of it from every angle. They got their colleagues to spread a tarp out, and they numbered each stone in turn as they disassembled the thing with enormous care rock by rock by rock.

In the cracks and crannies, they found all manner of trinkets and oddments. A man's pocket comb. A woman's brooch. An old worn brass belt buckle. What looked like an ivory button. A shoe heel weathered and walked thin. A fork with two tines missing. One half of a pair of pliers. An eye dropper with something inside it. What looked like a dried-up lemon peel. The skeletal paw of what would prove to be a possum, and one human big toenail—the entire thing.

There was nothing at the core of that stack of rocks, not truly even much of a hollow, and once everything was labeled and laid out in order, Flynn and them moved over to the fire hole and decided to sift all the ashes there. I'll admit I was about half bored by then.

There was enough of a crowd with me in the woods to keep me from feeling unduly anxious, and I found that watching competent people do their work in their competent way and impose their order on what had seemed wild and primal a little while before had the effect of flattening life out to make everything ordinary. Yes, of course sometimes people stacked rocks in the woods and made twig boxes full of feathers and hair ribbons. Ruiz would corral them presently, I told myself, and we'd get a fit explanation.

That's where I was as we left the woods and walked Ruiz down to the workshop. We'd left the doll with the heart drawn on it atop the bench in there.

"Y'all see much devil worship?" Ronnie asked Ruiz like he was asking her if she got a lot of rain out where she lived.

"Some," was what she told him, and then she touched on a couple of cases she'd either worked herself or had heard about. Only one of them didn't involve teens who'd gone depressed and gothic, and that one—by the sound of it—had been nearly as bent as ours.

"Perp was a financial advisor," Ruiz told us. "Invested money for churches mostly, and he was convinced Satan had come to him in a dream." According to Ruiz, Lucifer had taken the shape of a woman the financial advisor had previously dated.

"He told us they were engaged, but once I'd gone to see her, she said she could hardly remember who he was. She'd met him online through some lonely hearts church thing, some app. She was a regular at it, would get taken to dinner and then go home to her cats."

We were walking through the pasture grass, down beyond the pecan grove, and Ruiz by then had said more than I'd ever heard out of her, and I was reasonably sure I'd had sex with the woman very possibly twice. It could be Ruiz was as rattled as I was and had decided talking might help, or maybe she was working through local satanic sorts, ranking them in her head.

"He ended up killing his yard man. Slipped up behind him with a shovel. Said he thought it was that woman from before."

"That doesn't make a lick of sense," Ronnie said.

Ruiz nodded. "Now you're catching on."

We were nearly to the shed by then, and I felt sure I'd left that doll on the workbench right alongside the vice, but when I went in to fetch it, I couldn't find the thing.

"Over here, wasn't it?" I asked Ronnie.

Ronnie came in for a look and a nod. "Gone now."

Ruiz didn't strike me as interested enough, in any of it really. Granted she was professional law enforcement and I was just some guy, but we were closer to the same level than you might be somewhere else where "professional" meant professional. Our cops were chiefly knuckleheads happy to mix it up with drunks, and if you hung on long enough you could well find yourself in a sportcoat driving around in an unmarked Ford while you reduced a toothpick to pulp.

I got summoned to The Colon again that very night. Different room, but it looked just the same except the sheets were a touch shinier and thinner. No Turkey on this occasion, no conversation much. She pulled off her clothes and worked some at mine once I'd seemed (I guess) sluggish to her, and she headed me off when I started to ask her a question about the case.

Ruiz pressed an ink-stained finger to my lips and said by way of instruction, "Don't."

Then she made use of me and, I'll confess, I made some use of her. She was dressed and gone already by the time I came out of the shower. I got left to try to dry myself with a towel that had no nap.

8

Ronnie managed to dredge up semi-pertinent information because he had a whole network of people he'd given schwag to in the past. If somebody useful to Ronnie had need of a log splitter or a hydraulic jack, Ronnie would show up with one and, there in that moment, not ask for anything back.

"I'm always looking down the road," was how Ronnie chose to put it.

So he had sources he could tap, and while a few might have been reluctant because the stuff Ronnie had given them had turned out to be pilfered crap, enough had cause to be grateful and stood ready with their morsels. Consequently, we started building a fractured and half-assed mosaic out of the sorts of details Ruiz could have readily given me nights at The Colon if she'd only believed for a second that I was worth confiding in.

I worked on her. Ronnie insisted, but she told me precious little, and I wasn't sure I could much blame Ruiz since even I didn't really care for the version of myself that showed up at the Colon some nights. Not every night. Not nearly often enough for me. Sometimes we'd skip a week, and I'd catch myself getting blue and mopey until Ruiz would find me. She'd just text the time. "8," she'd say. And I'd wait before I gave her a "k" since I didn't want to come off as eager.

So there I was neck-deep in a mystery with a romantic angle to it, but the mystery smelled of the slaughterhouse, and the angle left me antsy and ill. I tried to talk that stuff out with Ronnie once, but he was all about the sexual details. He cut me off to describe an activity that he claimed to get up to with Sugar. It sounded like half fraternity hazing and half Chinese acrobatics.

I gave Ronnie an idea of the sort of sex Ruiz preferred, which was not gymnastic in the least (Chinese or otherwise) and was more about friction. Sometimes the woman seemed to be hoping to start a fire.

Ronnie listened without comment. What could you say? People do what they do, most especially girls.

So our intelligence was coming from Ronnie's folks chiefly and what we could get out of Casper and Janet. They'd become friendly with Grimes, of all people, who'd owned up to an avid interest in campervanning, and he'd swing by to hear their travel tips and pour over their gazetteer.

It was Grimes who gave us (by way of Casper) a nugget about the Galloway who owned the farm with the pecan grove. As far as the cops knew, he was still alive somewhere.

"Found three addresses," Grimes told Casper, "but he ain't at any of them."

Ronnie was acquainted with people who had personal knowledge of Galloways, the wrong Galloways the first two tries but the right ones the third time out. I was having to drive Ronnie around since he wasn't a Sherlock with a car, which meant we fit everything between my jobs, and Ronnie fussed with me about it.

"You want to catch these people, don't you?" he asked me more than once.

"Yeah, but I want to eat too" is what I usually told him. Then he'd acquaint me with the virtues of being your own boss and having a freelancer's schedule.

"Look at me," he'd say. "Freedom to innovate." I'd usually keep myself from reminding Ronnie he was just a thief.

So he'd complain about my workload as I drove him all over the place to talk to people about Galloways and, eventually, to talk to Galloways themselves. Ronnie's network came through for him and put us together with that farm-owning Galloway's niece in a fairly short time. She lived two counties over and agreed to meet us in a Baptist church playground.

Her name was Dawn, and she was minding a trio of toddlers who, somehow, all seemed to be hers. Me and Ronnie had decided we could stand to gussie up those days when we were meeting with the public, and I took that to mean wear jeans that smelled washed and a proper shirt with buttons, but it got to where Ronnie would only ever make calls on civilians in his suit. He just had the green one, and Ronnie was proud of it in a dogged and diligent sort of way. He'd picked it up at a place on the interstate where they'd had to mark it down twice to shift it, and Ronnie liked that he'd saved big cash just by being hard to please. He didn't care that he'd ended up with a suit you might see on a stage in Vegas, and nobody we talked to ever said a thing about it.

That was kind of how it went in the countryside. People took you as you came, which didn't remotely indicate approval. They just lacked the energy to grapple with your mess and figured you were free to be a fool if that's what you really wanted.

So Ronnie's suit out there in the churchyard got no rise from that Galloway who talked to us between bouts of curbing and correcting her children. They kept throwing dirt at each other no matter how loudly she told them, "Hey!"

We described the farm to her, Ronnie did anyway and showed her the map we'd printed.

"Yeah, that's it," she told us. "Uncle Foy had piles of cows."

"What happened with your uncle?" Ronnie was asking all the questions. There was a brick wall through the churchyard, and I was letting it hold me up.

Foy's niece said, "Hey!" which seemed to satisfy her while still having no effect upon her children. They kept pushing each other and drooling on ants and taking turns flinging stuff and bursting into tears.

"He still alive?" Ronnie asked her.

She nodded. "Last I heard."

"Know where we can find him?"

"Hey!" She shrugged. "In a home somewhere. We didn't get on."

"Did he lease that farm to anybody, far as you know?"

"Why?" The woman got interested all of a sudden. "Somebody working it?"

"Not exactly," Ronnie told her and looked my way. For his purposes, I was sort of the backstory guy.

"You hear about that dead sheetrocker?" I asked Dawn the niece. "Stuck in a hole?" I jabbed my thumb in a southerly direction like maybe that would help her.

She appeared to be getting uneasy with us and shook her head the least little bit.

"They found him on your uncle's place," I told her.

"If he goes out there and falls in a hole, how's that anybody's trouble but his?"

"Somebody killed him," Ronnie said.

"When?"

"A couple of weeks back, and we were just wondering if your uncle might know who's out there on his farm."

"Cousins? Grandkids? Something like that?" I suggested to her.

"Was he shot, this sheetrocker?" Dawn asked us.

Green Sherlock did the right thing and asked, "Why?"

"Cause I might know a boy who's bad for using guns."

"Who'd that be?" Ronnie asked her.

"Hey!" Then she told us, "Cousin."

"Got an address for him?"

She kind of did. It was one of those routes that was a string of landmarks no human could possibly remember, but when she finished telling it all, Ronnie asked her, "Not the boy with the ear, is it?"

She nodded. "He needed a generator," Ronnie explained as we were walking back to my car. "I was able to help him out."

"He isn't one of those nutty veterans, is he?"

Ronnie couldn't be sure but didn't believe so. "I think just dumb and mad all the time. You know."

I was all for Ruiz and Grimes riding out to have a word with this boy, especially on account of how dumb and mad had gotten to be such a regular thing that it was hard to engage with people anymore without stuff getting sparky. But Ronnie had put on his green suit, we were in the vicinity. He even knew pretty much where to find the guy without following any landmarks at all.

Ronnie directed me to what often passes out in the country for a bar, which was just a house on a two-lane road where the owner lived upstairs and everything below was counters and tables, two or three refrigerators, beer signs that lit up, and carpet you hated to touch with the soles of your shoes. Like most of them, this one didn't have a name beyond "Tavern" that somebody had written on a box flap and stuck in a window. There were two motorcycles out front and a pickup held together with strategically riveted strips of sheet tin.

What I said to Ronnie was, "Man, I just don't know," but Ronnie reminded me that the sort of folks we'd run into in that bar were almost sure to be his kind of people. I took him to mean chiselers with morals of convenience who'd recognize Ronnie, even in his green suit, as one of theirs to the bone.

"We're coming from a funeral," Ronnie told me by way of prep. "Your momma, or somebody, died."

"How come I'm not wearing a suit?"

"Cause y'all didn't get along. You weren't even supposed to go, but you went anyway."

"To my own momma's funeral?"

But Ronnie was halfway inside by then. That place was what I'd expected except for smelling appreciably worse. Powerful man stink, fry grease, the sweet reek of stale, spilled beer. The TV was tuned to a game show where people appeared to be trying way too hard to win a lifetime supply of moonpies. There was a bartender in a t-shirt with a big red dollar sign on it, and he appeared to have gotten around to removing only one of the sleeves. He had three patrons, and two were busy disagreeing about something while the third guy was working on his Hi-Life bottle, trying to ease off the label in one piece.

Ronnie knew the bartender, as it turned out. Or, more to the point, the guy knew Ronnie and so greeted him and me a little by saying, "Well, look here."

Those two shook hands in some funky, fraternal way, and then Ronnie glanced at me. "Just coming from his mamma's funeral."

In the slot Ronnie left, I told the guy, "We didn't get on."

I didn't get called upon to elaborate because the two boys who'd been disagreeing decided just at that moment they'd probably rather kill each other instead. They knocked over their table along with all the stuff sitting on it and then rolled around on the filthy tavern floor.

The bartender looked far more exasperated than alarmed, and he came out from behind his makeshift counter and, instead of telling those two to break it up, he kicked the pair of them by turns and for a while. They didn't appear to much care and kept on rolling around and punching until the bartender managed to boot them out the door and let them fight on the stoop if they wanted.

I ended up paying for two beers and left Ronnie to

work that bartender however he saw fit. They re-lived old times they'd had, which from what I could hear had been given over to larceny and dirttrack racing, and it seemed the bartender had married and then divorced a girl Ronnie had gone around with, so they took turns talking about her in a most unflattering way.

Ronnie got down to business after a while. In fact, he was kind of deft at it, most especially for a lowlife thief in a bright green suit. He managed to drag that Galloway into things without bringing their chat to a halt.

"You talking big Foy?" the bartender asked him.

"Don't know," Ronnie said. "One with the farm."

"Down by the river?"

Ronnie nodded.

"Why? What's going on down there?"

I'd found it was common with country people to make everything conditional. They'll fill you in most likely, but they want to know the outlines first. Who's making out. Who's taking a beating. What exactly is the upside of talking.

Moreover, that bartender knew Ronnie well enough to be sure he was up to something.

"Got my eye on some stuff," Ronnie told him.

"What stuff?"

"A John Deere harrow and a big pile of walnut planks."

The bartender nodded like he approved of the haul.

"I go back with Galloways, so it isn't like I'd stick it to them."

I feared Ronnie was pushing the limits, honor among thieves and all that, but the bartender saw nothing queer about any of it and told Ronnie, "Talk to Danny."

"Big fellow, right? Missing most of one ear?"

That earned Ronnie a nod.

"Know where we can find him?"

"Sure do." The bartender pointed. "He's over at the stove."

Then he shouted, and a guy came out of what passed for a kitchen. He was wearing a filthy apron and an ancient, moth-chewed top hat.

Danny Galloway recalled Ronnie only well enough to point at him there at first, but then the details all came flooding back once Ronnie said, "Generator."

For my part, I was slipping looks at the side of Danny Galloway's head trying to figure out what might have happened to his ear. He only had the top third left and nothing but scrap below it. It looked chewed and maybe chemical burned as well.

Danny begged off briefly so he could go fetch what he had going in the fryer, which proved to be chicken hearts and gizzards along with bits of fatback, and those boys wrestling on the stoop must have smelled it from outside because they gave up the battle and came straight in. They even ordered fresh beers for the house

before picking up the table they'd knocked over and set-
tling in for a feed.

We got offered some hearts and gizzards as well, but
I couldn't get past the aroma. Old fry oil and probably
older chickens mixed with pig from God knew when, so
I made out to be too sad about my momma to eat.

We'd gone there thinking maybe that Galloway with
the piece of ear might be in with devil crew or at least
know something about them because the niece with
the toddlers had led us to think he was exactly the right
kind of bent, but we came to find out he was merely a
gun nut who drew pleasure from shooting chickens.
Other people's chickens for sure, so he was an outlaw
no doubt, but he'd no more thought about Satan lately
than he thought about the Treaty of Versailles.

As long as you weren't a Rhode Island Red, he was
decent company. He didn't know anything about the
stuff going on out on big Foy's farm. In fact, he hadn't
been down there in more years than he could count.

"Believe I was nine," he told us. "Copperhead bit me
one night." He pulled down his sock and showed us his
leg where the venom had gone in. He couldn't think of
anybody he knew who had much truck with the devil
or, truth be told, any use for Jesus at all.

Finally, once he was about to head back to the kitch-
en, I asked him what had happened to his ear, and at
first, he told me it was a gator. Then he said it was pi-

rates before he confessed to having run with a woman who proved to be deranged.

"Could have been your pecker." Ronnie was one for looking on the bright side.

That Galloway joined him there, after a fashion. "Left me enough to hold up my hat."

Ronnie wondered out loud why the girl with the toddlers was so very down on Danny.

"Easy," was what he said back. "Middle one's mine."

By the time we got home, we'd been all afternoon chasing around just to find out the Galloway we were after lived in a care home somewhere or another and even the people who'd known him couldn't half remember him anymore.

"Got to be a better way." That was Simpson telling Sherlock that we wouldn't be riding the roads to reel in next to nothing again.

As it turned out, though, the professionals weren't doing any better, which I got a report about far sooner than I would have guessed. And not because I went to The Colon. I'd decided to steer clear of the place. Actually, I'd decided to decide not to go there anymore, since I do everything in stages. I only knew I didn't like the way I felt when I came out.

That left me planning to tell Ruiz I wasn't a motor lodge sort of guy, but fortunately for me, I never did have to because she showed up at my place a night or two later, just parked right in front of the house in her sedan, came straight up and let herself inside.

"Got decent sheets?" she asked me straight off.

"Some in the cupboard," I told her.

"Put them on."

It was immediately better to be in my own bed looking up at my own ceiling instead of fidgeting on a motel mattress eyeing their knotty headboard and wondering about the traffic that room had seen.

Being at my house, though, didn't serve to change Ruiz at all. She did what she felt like she needed to and got what she'd decided she wanted, and I was there to witness the whole thing without being involved much at all.

"What have you got to eat?" she asked me during the intermission.

"A pork chop from ... a while ago. About half a tub of cheese puffs."

"That's it?"

"Cornflakes. I'd need to sniff the milk."

"How old are you?"

I lied and told her, "Thirty-six."

"Got family?"

"Not really."

"So nobody left to disappoint?"

"If that's how you want to look at it."

She nodded and said, "It is."

I sulked briefly. The older I get, the more I seem inclined towards sulking. "I'm just kind of in a rut," I finally confessed.

"Get out of it," Ruiz told me and then went off to the kitchen to check my refrigerator and cupboards for herself.

When she came back, she got up to what she apparently thought of as snuggling, which meant we were side by side on our backs with our shoulders kind of touching, I told her where me and Ronnie had gone, who we'd talked to, and what about. "Big Foy, they call him. He's in some home near Roanoke."

"Yeah," she said. "We called. We heard."

She and Grimes had chiefly (as it turned out) been chasing around in a different direction. They had run down surveillance footage of diaper guy going on the lam in Petersburg.

"A girl came for him. Said she was his granddaughter."

"They didn't get her ID or anything?"

"Not a big market for incontinent geezers, but the camera picked up her tag.

"That's good."

"Car's stolen."

"Oh."

"What are you learning here?"

"This stuff's sort of...complicated?"

Ruiz nodded. "So you and captain underpants might want to just back off."

"But he's got a suit and everything."

"So take him to the prom."

Once I'd told her I'd talk to Ronnie, Ruiz rolled my way and laid her cheek against my chest.

"Now lay still and be grateful."

That sounded like something I could probably do.

9

Becky was one of those bosses who lived for her employees letting her down since that worked to confirm Becky's low opinion of people. To her way of thinking, we were all hopeless kleptomaniacs with no detectable initiative, a crew of ingrate knuckleheads she only kept on at the diner because she couldn't find a way to do every stinking thing herself.

Becky wasn't much nicer to the customers, but folks appeared to have decided that was part of the charm of the place. They could come in for a helping of canned green beans, a hunk of salty meatloaf and get as well a side of belittling, snide remarks from the owner. Double D's was kind of like Hooters in reverse.

If you missed a shift or were late for one or needed to beg off a day or two, there was zero chance you'd have a useful conversation with Becky. Instead, you were almost certain to get chuffed and snorted at, sometimes fired, but she'd almost always have to take you back since the pool of local people who'd work for Becky was small and ever shrinking because her fuse was widely known to be as short as her jeans were tight.

It was a bit worse for me due to how I couldn't tell Becky much of what I'd been up to. "Sort of helping the police," was as far as I'd go since I knew anything I said she'd broadcast and spread around.

So I'd give her sketchy details and tell her I'd been doing "things".

"What things?"

"Can't say. They made me sign a paper."

"What kind of paper?"

"You know, the kind that keeps me from saying what things."

That invariably went over poorly with Becky who, though she was down on everybody, had a particularly low opinion of lawyers, who she had to believe had drawn up the paper that would make a dishwasher shut up.

Of course, I told Rochelle the entire business because he was a sane man with a reliable sense of the world. The world anyway as it existed between Virginia and Alabama.

"People'll read the Bible wrong and get up to crazy stuff" was Rochelle's basic pronouncement on the matter, and then he launched into "I'll Fly Away."

Ruiz came to see me at Double D's right at the shank of lunch service one day, and Becky told me through the service window, "Lady here for you," and then went on to inform me she wasn't running some kind of social club where my friends could swing by and get free cobbler and stuff.

Ruiz had a photograph from a surveillance camera, had four or five of them actually from around the place in Petersburg where diaper guy had been living. A girl had walked him out of there and driven him off. That was perfectly clear from the pictures, and she was a normal-looking young woman who took care to buckle him up in a Nissan with Ohio tags.

"Don't recognize her, do you?" Ruiz asked me once she'd finished complaining about the mug of Double D's coffee she'd ordered. "Put it back in the battery," was her advice to Becky as she shoved the cup away.

"No," I said, but I did notice a couple of things. First, that the girl was gentle and easy with diaper guy and didn't appear to be much worried that somebody might come out and stop her.

"How's he fixed for granddaughters?"

"Got two, but they're not her."

"And the car?"

"Stolen from an outlet mall parking lot. Burlington, NC."

I did feel a morsel smarter in a glancing sort of way since I had evidence there on the lunch counter of what a fool you'd have to be to expect to go much of anywhere out of camera range. That seemed to be how Ruiz and her ilk found out almost everything. A crime happened, and they'd roll back the tape until they saw who did it.

That's why a man like Grimes could have a going career as a county detective since, aside from toothpick chewing, he just needed to sit and watch.

"Have you thought at all about why?" I asked Ruiz.

"Not yet," is what she told me.

And that was the thing about knowing who and where and how from cameras all over. The only bit they didn't supply was why. It seemed to me things had just about reached the point where it didn't matter if I'd killed a man because we'd quarreled or if I was just sour and ruthless and he was handy to get dead. Neither one made it worse for me or better at all for him. Cops had footage. I'd done what they'd seen. What else did they need to know?

"I think about why," I told Ruiz. "Kind of a lot, I guess."

"We need who first," is what she said back, and then she tapped on the stack of photos. "Show them to your boyfriend. Find out if he's ever seen her."

I didn't want to tell Ruiz that Ronnie had lately gone on a bit of a thievery spree and so wasn't at that moment handy for Sherlocking.

A crew had been mowing the interstate median and had left their tractors out overnight, and Ronnie had seen them while he was riding back from the Home Depot with Sugar. Those two had gotten rambunctious and busted some floorboards under Ronnie's mattress. Since he was worried about what might join him from the crawlspace in the night, off they went to get planks and a saw, some nails and also a clawhammer. Like usual, Ronnie had tossed the stuff over the fence in the garden shop and then checked out at the register with AA batteries and a load of chat.

Ronnie believed that if he had a receipt because he'd actually purchased an item then he could hardly be stealing the stuff he'd found in the side lot over the fence.

It worked out fine on this occasion. It all fit in Sugar's car, and then they came across those mowers on a stretch of highway where a man who knew the territory could get one of those tractors up a side road and hide it for a while. Ronnie parked it by an old sawmill nobody had used for years and covered the thing with branches and rusty sheet tin, was figuring on letting it sit until VDOT gave up and made a claim.

Ronnie was committed to the idea that his luck always hit in runs, so after the Home Depot caper and the articulated mower, Ronnie went on kind of a binge. That's how he got tangled up with a deputy a county over who stopped Ronnie because he was hauling a life-sized fiberglass steer on a stolen rollback truck. The steer was on the truck when Ronnie took it, and the straps were all seized at the ratchets, which Ronnie admitted later might have drained the stealth from the thing.

They locked him up, and the judge over there let him sit in a cell for nearly a week until Ronnie finally was permitted a call and put it in to Sugar who swung by my place in between clients to pass along the news.

"He's pinched pretty good," she told me. "Wants you to get hold of Thad."

Thad was Ronnie's lawyer and also his fence in a regular way since Thad had several addiction problems, usually sequentially. He'd go from pills to alcohol to gambling to cocaine and then occasionally to binge shopping before disappearing for six weeks to get clean. The rehab never really took with Thad because his clients were all Ronnie caliber, and they preferred, instead of cash, to pay the man in contraband.

Thad was deep into a cocaine phase when I finally tracked him down, and he said he had kind of a scumbag backlog to deal with before he could help Ronnie out, Ronnie who was sitting in the lockup because no bondsman would chance it with him. So Ronnie got to lounge around in orange coveralls and shoes with no laces and eat white bread and canned stew for a bit.

I went over to see him, took him socks and soap like he wanted, and because Ronnie never met a stranger, he'd made a couple of friends in jail. One was a meth head who claimed people called him Stiletto. That's what Ronnie told me anyway. Stiletto himself had so few teeth he could barely make himself understood. "You sure he's not saying Stanley?"

I asked Ronnie. Ronnie had been with the guy a week by then, but all he could manage was, "Oh."

He'd also gotten on good terms with one of his keepers, a deputy named Mason who looked exactly like a deputy named Mason ought to look. Baby fat. Weak chin. Hair in full retreat. Most of his colleagues got put on lockup duty by way of punishment, but Mason told Ronnie he usually volunteered.

"I don't much like it out there," was how Mason chose to put it. "You wouldn't believe some of the crap I've seen."

Ronnie was not only primed to believe it but might have even perpetrated a bit.

"Get this," Ronnie told me. "Some of that crap was a dead guy in a hole."

"Who? What kind of a hole?"

"Our kind."

"You sure?"

Ronnie told me he'd pinned Mason down on the thing, but instead of filling me in on the details, Ronnie just gave a whistle and Mason came in and told it all to me himself.

It was that kind of place, small and casual, not really built to be penal. They only had four cells, and the folks they brought in were ordinarily just passing through.

Not Ronnie though. He didn't just have trouble with the bondsmen. Ronnie confessed to me he might have stolen a stock trailer from the judge.

"It was three or four years ago," Ronnie said. "You'd think he'd have let it go by now."

So Mason came into the visitors' room, which was actually just a brief bit of hallway with a bench along it.

"Tell him," Ronnie said while pointing my way, "about that boy in the hole."

"Dead already," Mason told me. "They just stuck him in there?"

"Who?"

"Don't know."

"What kind of hole?" I asked him.

He described it with his hands. "Like you'd put a phone pole in."

"Dead how?"

"Beat a lot but strangled some too."

"Y'all got any idea who did it?"

"Naw," he told me, said it like that had never even been a possibility, as if him and his buddies weren't in the people catching business at all.

Then he had a thought and added, "There was this crazy-ass girlfriend, but she was off somewhere doing something else. I think they figured it was a bad sort that killed him, you know, probably passing through."

I'd heard that one plenty. We pinned most all of our

local ugly stuff on transient desperadoes, which had the effect of letting us out of wondering about ourselves.

"Got a file on this me and him could look at?" Ronnie even winked at Mason and then pointed my way with his forehead. "He's writing some kind of movie." And that was really all it took. People are daft when it comes to movies, and Ronnie knew how to pull the strings.

"Let me see," Mason said and went off to fetch what he could.

"Don't be telling your girlfriend," Ronnie advised me. "This is Sherlock shit right here."

Mason came back with an actual case file. "Ten minutes," he told us and put himself on lookout duty.

Ronnie took the photos and left me with the paperwork, so I told him the dead boy was a Duncan who drove a dozer for a paving crew.

"Says here he got along with people all right. No record. Church-league softball. Ex-wife. A couple of kids. Here you go. Crazy-assed girlfriend," I said.

Ronnie held up one of the photos, bare legs sticking out of the ground in a way that looked familiar.

"She's a Kirby," I told Ronnie. "Tamara Ann. Was either living out in Blackstone or is from there. Hothead sounds like." I read out to Ronnie all the charges the girlfriend had piled up, which tended to suggest, in aggregate, that she was powerfully lippy. She'd been nabbed for drunk and uncooperative, for failing to follow official instructions, for officer abuse. Resisting arrest. Like that.

Ronnie found a photo of her in with his stack of stuff. We figured it was her anyway because *Tamara* was spelled out in glitter on her shirt. She looked like trouble—big brown eyes and a pixie haircut, handsome enough to turn any man's head and, by the looks of her, energetic.

Then Ronnie showed me a picture of that dead Duncan boy. He'd been hosed off and was on a gurney somewhere, so the light was good and his wounds were clean, which made him less of a ghastly spectacle and more of a curiosity.

"What do you suppose would do all that?" It was the question that photograph begged because that Duncan had punctures in various spots but also places where his skin was battered and bruised and looked like it had just given way. He had a dingy ring around his neck as well like maybe he'd been strung up.

"If you were going to kill somebody," Ronnie asked me, "how many ways would you do it?"

I told him I'd probably be satisfied with one.

"They know this is a gang of people, right?" Ronnie shouted out to Mason, but Mason wasn't sure what anybody knew from one minute to the next.

"Who's Mona?" I asked Ronnie who put it to Mason. She figured into the paperwork throughout.

"His sister, I think. The dead guy."

"She in here?" Ronnie asked him, and Mason stepped away from his lookout spot to pluck a photo of her out of the pile.

She was mean looking. No pixie haircut for her, but iron gray braids that she'd twisted and piled on her head like a pair of snakes. She was what people call handsome when pretty won't begin to fit.

"Where'd they find him?" Ronnie asked, and Mason gave him road numbers and landmarks and told Ronnie where precisely a woman scratching around after morels had come across that Duncan boy shoved in his hole.

"Might as well look as long as you're here."

I told him I would, but I actually didn't intend to. Even after Mason followed me out to the lot to give me directions all over again, I was still thinking I'd drive off whichever way would satisfy him and then turn wherever I needed to get home.

But as it happened, that Duncan boy had been found dead just off the road I'd be traveling, and once I'd realized I wasn't likely to make it back without a pee, I turned off where Mason had told me to and parked where he'd suggested and right away found the track he'd said would take me to the spot.

It wasn't woods exactly but more like an overly ambitious thicket, sufficient to hide me while I relieved myself and yet not near enough of a forest for me to get worked up about. I worried about chiggers and reptiles, of course, but I can usually handle that and so pressed on ahead along the dwindling trail as the ground grew evermore boggy, and soon enough I reached the sycamore Deputy Mason had described in detail. It was growing at an angle and lightning-blasted at the top and had knobs on the trunk that seeped what looked for all the world like jelly.

The hole, of course, was long gone by then. That Duncan had died a little over a year back, so I couldn't even find police trash—the yellow tape, the paper booties—but just beer cans and busted liquor bottles left by locals come to see where some fool had bought it.

It was a grim spot even without me having to imagine a dead man plunged into the seepy ground. With every step I took, my footprints filled behind me with black water, and some kind of beetle the size of a nail head was biting me hard enough to draw blood. I would have given up and retreated but for the carving I'd been told to see. It was supposed to be on a chestnut limb that had gotten snared and cradled in a viney tangle, and I followed the trash and the wet, greasy path through the swampy scrub pretty much straight to it because the thing was apparently notable in the area and visited often by the sorts who tend to leave their cans and mess.

Deputy Mason couldn't remember what words exactly had been scratched into that limb. He felt like they had a picture of it somewhere, but it wasn't with the rest.

The rubberneckers, of course, had done more carving, so now that limb was a profane garble and had every kind of yee-haw-I've-been-right-here folks could think to put on the thing.

I learned that a girl named Kaylou was easy and available and boys named Frank and Jimmy weren't nothing but ignorant fools. I found *poontang* twice, and somebody with skill and leisure had carved a respectable Camaro onto the thing. Just off the front bumper was where I finally saw the word that mattered. It was "shall."

The wood on either side was all chewed up and carved over, so there were hardly any hints of what had gone before it and after. It could have been something from the good book or something from the Constitution, but I felt fairly sure it wasn't Kaylou related.

I had to think this was a spot Ruiz needed to hear about. So I called her from there in that boggy thicket, got her voicemail and called her again. I called her a third time, and she finally answered.

"Can't talk," she told me. "We got her."

"Got who?"

"You know," she said, "Diaper guy's blonde."

10

Thad managed to spring Ronnie with just a fine. He made it seem like Ronnie had been diagnosed with an affliction, and they hadn't quite gotten his medicine balanced right. So Ronnie hadn't realized the truck he'd climbed into wasn't actually his. It probably helped that Ronnie remembered seeing an articulated mower and was able to tell the deputies exactly where it was.

In my view, this was the best outcome Ronnie could conceivably hope for, but he did come home constipated and with a nasty jailhouse fungus.

"I wouldn't wash a dog," he told me, "in that shower over there."

At first, I couldn't get Ronnie to focus much on our dead sheetrocker because he was mad at his judge and let himself lapse into scheming to burn down the man's fishing camp. I knew the urge would pass because Ronnie lacked, as a rule, the drive to be vindictive.

Until he got over it though, there was no working with him, and I ended up talking to Casper across the road. Even Janet a little, notwithstanding that Janet had long made it plain she didn't care for me at all. She'd decided I was the one who'd shot a hole in their camper van, and I couldn't see the point of ratting out Ronnie for it.

"He came from Petersburg," I told Casper and Janet. "That fellow in your house." I proceeded to give them all I had and tried to do it in sensible order.

Casper and Janet knew precious little about the dead sheetrocker and had only heard vague mention from Grimes about the writing in the truck.

"Book of Revelation," I told them and quoted the verse. "Got to wonder who'd kill a man, stick him head-first in a hole, and then write a snatch of Scripture in maybe his blood."

Casper felt sure in all their camper van travels they'd never come across the pitch of scoundrel who'd do such a thing to a man, but Janet reminded him of a woman they'd met in one of the Dakotas who prayed to a coconut head she'd bought in Tampa as a child.

"She'd ask it for things," Janet told me. "If she wanted you sick and hurt and miserable, she'd talk to her coconut head."

Casper still couldn't place her, which Janet and I together found hard to believe.

Janet had decided Ronnie was on vacation at Myrtle Beach while he was sitting a county over in the lockup. It didn't matter that he'd come back pale and fungal.

Janet had a thing about Ronnie and always worked up excuses for him, which didn't make much sense given how little slack she seemed to cut everybody else.

The way Casper explained it to me, Ronnie reminded her of her brother who she'd fallen out with ten or twelve years before, and instead of mending things with him, she just went easy on Ronnie.

"This all sure sounds mean," was Casper's take.

Janet went with, "Funny how people do." Then she trotted out a verse from Proverbs that she nearly got right. "Trust in the Lord with all your heart and don't lean on your own understanding."

"In all thy ways acknowledge Him," I told her, "and he shall direct thy paths."

That earned me a glare from Janet. She tolerated being quoted at poorly.

Ruiz came to see me a night or two later. She'd just get to feeling like she needed a tweak, and she'd show up and let herself in. I'd laid in snacks since her first visit so I could have something on offer, but she'd yet to come peckish and would take from me just the occasional dram of bourbon that she'd knock back in the bedroom while she was inspecting my sheets.

They didn't need to be fine cotton or anything like that, but the fitted sheet had to grip at the corners. No exhausted elastic allowed, and Ruiz had a particular way she liked to see the flat sheet tucked, which I became accomplished at in an effort to please her.

The best she ever gave me for it was a nod and a "Nice job."

The sex was ok as sex goes, but it certainly wasn't spiritual or even glancingly romantic. She'd get what she needed and then would flop for a stretch in silence. Sometimes she'd revive and roll my way for another go, but usually she'd groan and go looking for her underpants and socks.

Her shoes had been made in Portugal. I'd had a thorough look at them once while she was in the bathroom inspecting the contents of my medicine cabinet. Ruiz didn't make any secret of it but called out to me as she peed, "You razor blades are just about all rust, and buy a new toothbrush, for fuck's sake."

There was no special insole or anything. Those shoes were simply hideous, and she appeared to wear them by choice. I couldn't see the profit in asking her why since, given Ruiz's lack of sentiment, I had to believe she could easily locate another man with grippy sheets.

She didn't make me inquire about the blonde girl they'd lately picked up because Ruiz had spent frustrating hours with her and the creature was much on her mind.

"Hasn't said a word yet," Ruiz volunteered. "She just sits there. Do you know how hard it is to say nothing with two cops hammering at you?"

I had to think I didn't since I was an obliging sort.

"We showed her all the surveillance stills. We know she's diaper guy's sister's daughter's ex-husband's brother's girl. What even is that?"

I tried to do the familial math but couldn't begin to swing it.

"We pull her out of her cell, she sits and says nothing, so we just put her back."

"Is this kidnapping or something?" I felt like I ought to chime in.

"You saw him under all that stuff. I'm going with 'or something'."

I did manage to get her to look at a picture on my phone before she left, a snapshot I'd taken of that carved up limb in the bog. The light was hitting it just about right, so you could make out "shall" pretty well if you knew where to look and had the patience to let it float up from the cuts and gouges.

"Yeah, Duncan. Heard about him," she said. "Ran with a rough bunch. Owed a lot of money. Word is somebody choked him out."

"Beat him too. We saw the file."

"We who?"

"You know." I did that nose pointing thing. Maybe at Skylab. Maybe at Ronnie's house. "A deputy up there gave it to us. Ronnie got to know him."

"He work the scene, this deputy?"

Mason was more of a guy you'd send to chalk tires or direct school traffic, but I still nodded and told Ruiz, "Think so."

"And you went out there?" Ruiz grabbed at my phone and flipped through the pictures I'd shot.

"They liked his girlfriend for it. He was known to beat her up."

"Big eyes? Lesbian haircut?"

That sounded close. I nodded.

"Alibied up."

I knew that, but in some thinking I'd done, I'd found a way to work around it. "Wasn't it that Duncan's sister that alibied her?"

Ruiz nodded.

"Y'all check on her? She looked kind of rough."

"He ran with a hard bunch. Owed a lot of money."

Ruiz always stood ready to discount stuff that happened out in the boonies where people got up to things no civilized humans would do. Pulled their own teeth with lamp cord and dressed all manner of wounds with poultices made from mustard and kerosine, dug their own landfills with loader buckets no matter what the county told them, and made trucks and cars and racing mowers out of stuff they found in their yards. Why wouldn't they kill a man if they'd failed to get back the money he owed them.

"What about the hole?" I asked her.

"That one looked like they tried to bury him but got shiftless and quit."

It hadn't seemed that way to me, but I was just a civilian with three jobs.

"What now with the blonde?"

Ruiz grunted, didn't know.

"Has diaper guy seen her?"

She shook her head. "Not yet."

"Might shake him up," I suggested. "Make him come around." I'd seen it happen at the cineplex and plenty on TV.

Ruiz told me, "Hmm," but in a good way, and then she stripped right out of the clothes she'd only just put on and announced that wasn't a bad idea and I was due for a reward.

Instead, I got more grinding, and, after a bit, Ruiz yelped once and flopped over.

That was a weird passage for me, as life episodes go. I can see it well enough now, but when you're deep inside it, everything's just one day bumping into the next. You're manning a Fryolator and then sometimes driving a school bus, sometimes sawing plywood, sometimes visiting crime scenes with a guy in a loud green suit and then on the odd night pleasuring a woman by getting a scrotal Indian burn.

Ruiz was plowing her own row over at the temporary PD where she, in fact, brought diaper guy in unannounced as a surprise to blondie. Ruiz showed me a scrap of video on her phone one night while we were in-betweening and sitting on my bed. Diaper guy looked healthier than when I'd last seen him. His face was fuller. His color was better, and if you'd spied him out and around, you wouldn't have suspected he'd lately been under most everything Casper and Janet owned.

The girl was sitting at a table in what had clearly been the lockbox room of the bank. Half the cubby doors were shut, but the rest were standing open, which nagged at me because I've got a thing for order. I couldn't imagine myself getting much at all done until I'd closed all those lockbox doors.

I watched Grimes extract and examine his toothpick and then shove it back in his mouth while that blonde girl sat there gazing (I guess) into the middle distance.

Then in came Ruiz steering diaper guy who was wearing a retiree get up and so looked like a regular man. He had a glance around just to see where he was and then noticed the blonde girl at the table who stared at him squarely back.

"Look at her," Ruiz told me, so that's what I did, and even on Ruiz's phone screen, the venom came right through.

"Hates him."

Ruiz nodded. "Now watch this."

Diaper guy made a noise that came across as warbling confusion, and then he pulled free from Ruiz's grip so he could unfasten his pants. He dropped them and urinated, didn't aim or anything but just leaked all over the place as he hung.

Ruiz and Grimes reacted like ordinary people would. Ruiz backed away to keep clear of splatter while Grimes got out of his chair and swore. Ruiz stopped the video on her phone once it showed the girl's expression plain.

"What is that?" she asked me.

There was no joy to it. It was not a smile of pleasure or amusement. It was tight, thin, satisfied. I'd smiled that way myself, and I stopped to think why and when before I knew to tell her, "Spite."

"He couldn't get out of there fast enough." Ruiz let the video run.

"What does Grimes think?" I asked her.

That was a joke we had between us. Grimes didn't do a lot of thinking, and when you'd press him for an opinion on pretty much any semi-thorny thing, he'd scratch his head, maneuver his toothpick, and invariably say, "Don't rightly know."

We'd boiled it down, so Ruiz just told me,

"Rightly."

She played the whole thing for me again so I could watch from end-to-end. The angle was good on the blonde, and I could see that she despised him in a way that impressed me as furious and intense.

"What do you know about him?" I asked her.

"Taught North American history. Twenty-two years on the job. House in Portsmouth. Wife, two kids. Both boys. No trouble with the law."

"And the girl?"

"She grew up near Suffolk." Ruiz stopped the video on her phone right as diaper guy was draining. "Lived maybe twelve miles from him."

I didn't mention Ronnie much when I was around Ruiz because, being a cop, she knew shiftless trash when she saw it, but those two were kind on the same frequency where it came to that case, so I decided to break with protocol and tell her, "Ronnie's got a theory."

Ruiz made a noise.

"He thinks it's all because these guys were probably shit."

"Shit how?"

"You know. Hard on women." I made a fist and showed it to her.

"And why exactly does he think this?"

"Because Ronnie's kind of a shit guy. Or was anyway years back. If I think about it, I might have been one too."

"Give me a for instance."

"I shoved a girl once. Hell, twenty years ago. Sort of bounced her off a wall. I was drunk and kind of mad all the time back then, but I still remember the look she gave me. She would have knifed me if she could."

"And that Duncan boy and Tito, they were you two only worse?"

"That's kind of what Ronnie's thinking. Guess I'm thinking it a little too."

"What about the devil and the piles of rocks and stuff?"

"Dressing it up. Don't want to come off low and trashy."

"So it's dead shit guys and fed up girls?"

I figured that rated a nod.

"Hmm," she said, and there almost wasn't any acid to it. "Duncan and Tito do have history, and blondie sure hates diaper guy. I'm not saying you're right," she told me. "I'm just not saying you're instantly wrong."

That was far better than I'd expected. "Ronnie tells me Sugar's got a line on the freaks around. You know Sugar, don't you?"

"Oh, yeah."

"We were thinking it might be good if you talked to her."

Ruiz tossed her phone onto my nightstand, which was often a kind of preamble to the two of us getting frisky. "Anything else I ought to do?"

"That room with the lockboxes in it? It'd be alright with me if you shut all those little doors."

"Why am I here again?" she wanted to know.

"Because I've got grippy sheets."

11

Sugar wouldn't talk to Ruiz, she told us. Not even about the weather because, to hear it from her, she'd had a pile of ugly times with cops.

"Not Ike," she said, "but some of the rest of them..." Sugar groaned and shook her head.

It turned out she wouldn't even talk to me and Ronnie unless we took her to a restaurant, and she had one all picked out. It had been The Wagon Wheel for a considerable while—a steak place with a fire pit—and then it sat empty for a year or two until a young couple down from somewhere bought it to open a farm-to-table spot that served stuff like sake roasted pork belly with whipped parsnips and micro mustard greens.

That incarnation didn't really catch on, so after a stretch of losing money, the owners reworked the fire pit, installed a salad bar, and it became a steak house once again, a steak house with tablecloths, a wine list that was all but upholstered, and a little fellow from Guatemala who'd come around and bring you bread. You went there on prom night or for a wedding anniversary, or if you needed to pump a professional woman and she required a fancy lunch.

Ronnie wore his green suit while I stuck with my jeans and blazer. The plan was to meet Sugar out there, but she couldn't get her Corolla started, so we swung by and picked her up at The Colon, as it turned out, along with Tuffy, her miserable dog.

Sugar had just come off an appointment, she told us, with a lineman for Dominion who liked nooners in a regular way and smelled of creosote.

She was wearing one of those outfits a wiry woman can get away with, all bare arms and naked legs well past her knees and cowboy boots with rhinestones on them. Sugar had even done her face. Her eyelids anyway, which were baby blue with sparkles. I feared Ronnie might crawl over the seat back just to get next to her while I drove because he spent the first few minutes telling Sugar how fine she looked, and Sugar sounded primed for a transaction.

"I'm right here, teeny," she said to Ronnie and slapped the seat beside her.

There wasn't much chance I could help myself. "Teeny?" I had to say.

"Tell him," Ronnie instructed Sugar, but she was busy unscrunching her panties or something and so didn't speak up quick enough for Ronnie who informed me, "It's like ironic, you know?"

I checked Sugar in the rearview. She gave me a wink

and shook her head.

That didn't go over with Ronnie who started working at his belt, and it was looking like I'd soon enough have a prostitute and her yappy dog in my backseat and a neighbor with his member on display up front, none of which impressed me as even remotely appetizing, so it fell to me to say to Ronnie, "Uh-uh. We're about to eat."

Ronnie paused and unhanded his zipper. "It's ironic," he said again.

I was quick to tell him, "Got it. Fine. All right."

But then Sugar, who was gazing at the landscape, came out with, "Teeny," in a dreamy sort of way, which kind of tore it for Ronnie who decided he'd endured quite enough ridicule, so out he came with little Ronnie and told me six or eight times, "Look."

The thing is, with nothing to compare it to, I couldn't tell if little Ronnie was monstrous or not. It was just lying there all by itself looking like something you'd turn up with a spade.

Ronnie was going, "See? Huh?"

I nodded like I was wowed while, in truth, I was having a sort of rolling philosophical moment about the general relativity of every damn thing. Was Ruiz, for example, more crusty and unsentimental than most women, or was she like the vast run of females, and I'd just never known her type? Was it common in other places for men to get pulverized with bricks and then stuck head-first in holes as some brand of object lesson? Did people stack rocks in the deep woods in any regular way elsewhere in the world?

I simply didn't know, and I thought of myself as semi-worldly. I'd been to New Brunswick once for about three hours because I was sick of driving through Maine, but I still felt like I was guilty of being hemmed in and parochial because I was too damn content merely knowing what I knew. That was the thing Ruiz had on me. I was acquainted with local malevolence while she was familiar with that stuff at scale.

Even still, I felt like I could tell with some degree of confidence that Ronnie was probably a medium at best, though he did grunt and struggle in a showy way as he tucked the thing back in.

We got a table on the back deck so Sugar and Ronnie could smoke, and we had a view of what had started out as the kitchen garden which appeared to be given over to squash and Johnsongrass anymore. These days they were all in on ribeyes and baked potatoes and brought with your dinner rolls a big pewter caddy that held a tub of ranch dressing and a vat of sour cream.

Sugar ordered the six-ounce ladies steak, two of them because she was famished while me and Ronnie split a Delmonico because we were cheap. Our plan was to try to fill up on salad, bread, and townhouse crackers. Then Sugar went and ordered herself a bottle of wine but told the waitress to bring her over a gin and ginger first.

"We can write this off," Ronnie leaned in and said to me discreetly.

I knew there wasn't going to be a "we" because Ronnie had already sidled up with a wink and given me a whole five dollar bill.

We only started talking local freaks once we'd visited the salad bar twice.

"Got panties on a lot of the boys around here. You'd be surprised," Sugar told us.

"You mean they go around in them?" Ronnie said.

When Sugar nodded, I went with, "Why?"

She had some ideas but no solid reasons. "Some of these boys like you to smack them around," Sugar told us. "Tie them up. Pee on them. Like that." Sugar could just as well have been talking about her golf game. She never stopped eating as she filled us in and drained several glasses of wine. "And I used to have one that liked to choke me hard, but who needs that?"

"Any punchers?" Ronnie asked.

Sugar nodded. "But that's a one-time thing, and they pay me double, or I go straight to the law."

"Gone to the law?"

Sugar nodded my way.

"On who?"

"Fellow up by Jasper. Can't call his name. Smacked

me right here." Sugar tapped her left cheek. "Got all weepy once I'd laid into him for it. They do a lot of that. Try to knock you around and then blubber about it. Try to rape you sometimes and then cry like a damn baby."

I figured a couple of hours with Sugar was liable to put me off men altogether, which might make it tougher to go around being one.

"Did you know this guy Tito?" Ronnie asked her. "Sheetrocker that got killed?"

"Know a girl who knew him. Remember Darcy with the bangs."

Ronnie turned to me and explained that Darcy was kind of a load, and he'd been with her twice before he'd decided he probably preferred them bony.

"She's all some of them want," Sugar told us. "They like that big old behind of hers."

"Tito?" I asked.

Sugar nodded and forked a hunk of steak into her mouth as big around as a fifty-cent piece. It took three tries for Sugar to tell me the thing I wanted to hear.

"She said he half killed her. Might have finished the job if she hadn't hit him with a lamp."

"You didn't know a Duncan, did you? Would have been up near Blackstone."

Sugar told me she never had cause to work up there. "Do all right close to home." She winked at Teeny, and he fairly gurgled.

"Anybody else?"

"There's a Simmons," she told me, "out past the Lutheran church. He can't get himself stirred to go if you don't let him switch you across the legs with a piece of forsythia bush."

"Anybody worse?" Ronnie put to Sugar.

"Doodle. You heard of him?"

I hadn't. Ronnie neither. Or rather the Doodle Ronnie knew was not the Doodle Sugar meant. Ronnie's Doodle bagged groceries at the Kroger, and most people just called him Chief, while Sugar's Doodle lived out west in the county where he, apparently, was known for his temper and his cruel streak.

"Used to fight all the time, but he got old," Sugar told us. "Beat all the women he knew, so he had to start hiring out. Then he had a stroke or something and wasn't much trouble anymore."

"He one of yours?" Ronnie asked.

"Sometimes. He's a ten-minute handjob these days, but he went off somewhere a couple of weeks back, and nobody's seen him around."

"What do you mean 'went off'?" I asked her.

First, she had to send the Guatemalan guy after more sour cream, and then Sugar had trouble picking the dates she needed for her story. She couldn't decide if he'd gone off on a Tuesday or if maybe it had been a Monday instead, which didn't make a lick of difference.

I have to say, Rochelle is maybe my only acquaintance who knows how to come out with a story. That's one of the things I like about him most. He puts the details all in order, and he never backtracks to decide if something happened on Friday morning last or at the dawn of humankind because Rochelle has editorial sense and knows what doesn't matter. Sugar, though, was a lot more ordinary and treated everything the same, so I waited until she'd worked through her various calendar issues, and then she got tangled up with Ronnie on where exactly her Doodle lived, which sounded to have a lot to do with an old Sunoco station and what side of a smelting chimney out in the county it might be on.

I was finishing my roll and trying to figure what the check might end up being by the time Sugar finally got back around to how long her Doodle had been gone.

"Saturday," she said. "Three weeks ago now. I was swinging by to see him, and a neighbor boy told me they'd all been wondering where he went."

"With a stroke?" is what I asked her.

"He could walk all right," Sugar said. "Drive a little too, but his car was sitting out there in his yard."

"They find him yet?" Ronnie wanted to know.

Sugar shrugged. "I got kind of busy. Ya'll's sap gets up something awful sometimes."

I caught myself nearly asking Sugar how in the world she did it. She made no bones about being a pro and trading her virtue for pay, but even still I was acquainted with the strain of local man likely to rent Sugar's affections. They were guys you'd want to HazMat up to touch, and yet Sugar went at those boys in pretty much the altogether and accomplished for them whatever they'd decided that they'd bought.

I had to think it was probably like cleaning fish. The guts and the scales were off-putting, but once you'd done it enough, you just stopped paying much mind.

The check finally arrived, reached me once Ronnie and Sugar had both pointed my way, and the sum was staggering enough to prompt from me a Bible verse.

"The little that a righteous man hath," I said, "is better than the riches of the many wicked."

"Is he some kind of preacher?" Sugar asked Ronnie.

Ronnie said, "Yeah, some kind."

I got back to the car to discover that Tuffy had gnawed the cover off my steering wheel.

The plan was that me and Ronnie would ride out and nose around at Doodles, just on the outside chance the hickory nut crowd had done him harm. That seemed unlikely to me. The guy was feeble and afflicted, so he'd probably only wandered off and got lost in the woods.

We even talked about going straight over from lunch, but then Ronnie got sleepy, and we agreed to put it off. That meant I was available to fill in on a bus route even though I had a quarter cup of Sambuca in me, which

might have been the right amount since the load I carried was powerfully stirred up. Something had gone on
over at the middle school that had gotten them agitated. Somebody had broken or maybe gotten together or
some girl the boys were hot on had possibly changed
her hair.

I just kept to the route and let them do what they
wanted behind me, checked the mirror every now and
again in case a homicide was underway. And these were
civilized kids for the most part. A few of them were
known to be decent students, and they were raging
around back there like life for them had gone unhinged.

Given that civic order and lawfulness largely depend
on voluntary restraint, I wondered what we would do
when grown-ups decided to behave like middle schoolers and cut loose and do any damn thing they pleased.

That's the sort of stuff that was going through my
head by the time I got home and realized the only beer I
had was still that skunky lager, and I was sitting on the
toilet like I do sometimes, with my pants up and the lid
down—it's a welcome spot for contemplation—when
Ruiz knocked once and let herself on in.

"You here?"

I was not in a mood for her until I'd stepped into the
back hall and saw she'd brought a fresh bottle of Turkey. She had it in hand and a ratty bundle of paperwork
under her arm. Police stuff (I could see well enough),

photos mixed in with reports.

She could tell I was gloomy. I sure wasn't trying to hide it.

"What's on your mind?" she asked me.

"Aw, you know. Kids today."

I was afraid we'd end up in my bedroom, and I was in no state for that, both emotionally and in terms of my bed linen, so I was relieved to follow Ruiz into my kitchen instead.

She cleared my dinette by knocking my big sack of coupons onto the floor. I tear them off and cut them out and then leave them all at home, so it hardly mattered where they ended up.

I have just one ice tray, and Ruiz discovered I hadn't refilled it, so she threw it in the general direction of the sink, and then she had a look in my fridge and told me, "Jesus, stop buying jerky, and you don't need to put it in here anyway." She slammed the door. "That's kind of the whole point."

"Me and Ronnie pumped Sugar at lunch," I told her.

"Anything good?"

"Sounds like there's a Doodle we need to find."

"So find him," she said and gave me three sheets of paper clipped together.

It was results from Flynn and his chirpy colleague. I could see that well enough, but there were charts and columns of numbers that didn't mean a thing to me. I flipped through the pages anyway and made a show of being diligent and attentive.

"Bloodwork. Prints. Hair. We're getting it all now."

That sounded encouraging. "Who do you like?"

"Hard to say. Nobody much is really popping." Then Ruiz went through the results with me and showed me the mugshot of a woman. She looked familiar, had salt and pepper hair hanging down and what looked like a dragon tattooed on her neck. She had a mouse under her right eye and stitches in her bottom lip.

"Mona, that dead Duncan's sister. Pulled a print out at the farm. She got pinched a couple of years back for setting a guy's truck on fire."

"Oh, right. Her. Print where?"

"Back in that shed where you found that doll."

So Sherlock and Simpson had managed to do a glancing spot of good.

"And the writing's in blood, but it's only part human. The rest of it's *felis silvestris*."

I waited until she'd obliged me.

"That would be bobcat," she said.

"Weird."

"Yeah."

"When did it get too hard just to shoot a guy?" That sort of thing has worked for years."

That was too far-ranging for Ruiz who just shrugged.

"Where does this Mona live?" I asked her.

"Don't know, and she changed her name. Filed papers and everything." Ruiz handed me the document, but it was lightly printed and hard to read.

"Iphigenia," she told me. "Daughter of Agamemnon. Last name's now Orestes. Son of Agamemnon. Iphigenia means "strong-born" or something like it. Orestes means...can't remember, but he killed his mother."

I confessed to Ruiz that I had kind of a soft spot for brainy women.

"Hope you find one," she told me. "I just look shit up."

Then she did that thing where she kicked off her ugly shoes by way of seduction and foreplay before unsnapping her trousers and telling me, "Let's go."

Like Ronnie, I've got at least a trace of romance in my bones, so I have to think both of us have chosen poorly. Circumstances anyway have put us with women who do what they do without requiring from me or Ronnie even a vaguely tender gesture. Just cigarettes or bay rum in his case and laundered sheets in mine.

So I had to tell Ruiz I needed a couple of minutes to fix the bed.

She nodded as she unbuttoned her blouse, and before I left the kitchen I was thinking I ought to congratulate her on the fine police work she'd done, but she saw me lingering and asked me, "You still here?"

12

When I shared all the news with Ronnie, he jumped to sympathizing with the bobcat.

"No damn telling what they did to him."

I gave him the fullest account I could of Iphigenia Orestes, formerly Mona Duncan.

"They won't find her." Ronnie seemed certain. "That girlfriend of yours won't even half look."

"She's not my girlfriend, and why the hell not?"

Ronnie glanced around like there was a chance of us getting overheard there on his glider.

"Women throw in together," he said. "They can't help it. It's just something they do."

"She isn't like that," I told Ronnie in what, for me, was a show of pique.

Whenever I'd got short with him, Ronnie would take time to wonder aloud what sort of fix I might be in if he'd not helped a brother. Then he'd mention Gail and her boyfriends along with his gift of a rollaway bed, which was (in his view) inexhaustible as neighborly gestures go. So there hardly seemed much way that I could ever quit my Sherlock, though I did manage to put off carrying Ronnie out where Doodle lived for a while.

I had to think Ruiz was well on her way to button-
ing the whole business up. She had blondie in the lockup, and they were onto Iphigenia/Mona. Once Ruiz had
gotten them both inside, one of them was sure to crack.
That's how I figured it anyway, so when Ronnie made
noises about Doodle, I'd put him off or carry him somewhere closer by.

One evening I drove him to the pool hall where we
ate a bowl of cracklins and chatted with Queenie. She
appeared to take to Ronnie, partly because she liked his
suit and probably also because Ronnie was the same
with everybody. Better still, Queenie was exactly Ronnie's type—wiry and forceful enough to beat him up in
a pinch.

"Ruiz been in?" I asked a time or three before Queenie got around to nodding.

"What do you think it is with those two?" Ronnie
wanted to hear from Queenie.

And she said, "Well," and then told him considerably
more than she'd ever said to me, and I'd stopped in a few
times to try to cultivate the woman.

"She acts tough, but it's just a front."

"That's what I figured," Ronnie said. "Didn't I?" he
put to me.

Ronnie had a wealth of opinions about, well, almost
everything, so it stood to reason that some time or an-

other he might have proposed that about Ruiz.

"He's been getting over Gail. Hear about her?"

"I know a Gail," Queenie said.

"You wouldn't know this one," Ronnie assured her. "His Gail's trash."

So I got to sit there tugging on a long neck and munching on fried fatback while Ronnie shared with Queenie and everybody within earshot the sorriest possible version of my relationship with Gail. The more Ronnie talked and the more Queenie heard, the surer she got that the Gail she knew was my Gail after all.

"You hearing this?" Ronnie asked me. "Ain't this a tiny world?"

Better still, Queenie didn't necessarily like the Gail she knew, so she and Ronnie had a high time taking the hide off the woman and then wondering, in my presence, what kind of man she could possibly snare.

"I was in a rough patch," I explained to them both. "And it's not like she's bad looking."

Queenie glanced at Ronnie for his assessment of Gail's allure, and Ronnie shook his head and told her just, "Big-boned."

"That girl lies about everything," Queenie said as she fetched two more beers and gave them to us on the house.

It's not often that you get to sit and watch a romance blossom, especially one I suspected would end poorly.

Queenie was organized, appeared to be tidy, was running a going business, and was black while Ronnie was a white-trash rascal and layabout who thieved for a kind of living and, in humid weather, couldn't even open his front door.

I wanted to say, "Y'all just hold what you've got." But who among us hasn't reached for a thing just because there it sat?

So I drank and watched as I steadily became borderline invisible to them. I didn't tell Queenie that Ronnie probably needed fumigating, and I didn't mention to Ronnie a manfriend of Queenie's I'd seen hanging around. He was big and black and keen enough on the woman to snap Ronnie right in half.

I failed to bring up any of that and instead sat and endured their discussion of my relationship with Ruiz.

"She just needs it sometimes," Queenie declared. "We all do, but she's cut and dried about it. Doesn't get mushy. Doesn't ever get sweet. Wants what she wants and has at it."

"I knew she was one of them right from the jump," Ronnie informed Queenie. "Tried to tell him." Ronnie pointed my way, chiefly with his ear.

"You know how people are," Queenie said.

That was music to Ronnie. If he said something like that once a day, he said it fifty times.

"We're going to solve this thing," Ronnie informed

Queenie, "before that girlfriend of his gets to it."

"Wouldn't want to bet against her."

"Yeah, but look here," Ronnie said and leaned Queenie's way. "I've got kind of a gift."

"Ah," was what she went with. "What else have you got?" Queenie asked him just as a guy down the bar waved money for a fresh beer.

While Queenie was away, Ronnie leaned close to assure me that if the word "teeny" passed my lips, the two of us would tangle for sure.

When she got back, Ronnie asked her, "What time you get off?"

"Why?" Queenie asked.

"He's just naturally curious," I told her.

"Yeah," Ronnie said. "There's almost nothing I don't want to know."

Then he did that thing where he stuck his tongue in the gap where he'd lost an incisor. Ronnie seemed to think it was bewitching. Queenie, for whatever reason, appeared to think so too.

I drove home alone and very nearly put in a call to Ruiz until I'd paused long enough to reflect on all that Queenie had said about her. How unromantic she was to her core, practical and never needy, and I knew already if there was something I could do for the woman, she would have been on the phone to me. So I didn't call her but wandered around the house instead. I failed to sleep awfully much and ended up maybe at four-ish randomly opening my father's Bible and reading about Ruth and Boaz until I heard Casper (I felt certain) yelling in the road.

I pulled on some pants and went out on the porch to find Casper on the pavement with a flashlight and a pipe wrench. He was wearing the kind of underpants you might see on a beach in France. They were a sight on Casper who'd long since relaxed into a plush camper-van physique.

"Kids," he told me and pointed up the road with his wrench. "Out here messing with my van."

I followed him to his driveway where he shined his light on his quarter panel. Words written with a finger is what it looked like but with less skill than I'd seen before. There were drips and shaky penmanship.

"What does that say?" Casper asked me. "The whippoorwill?"

Not quite. I read it out to Casper. "The whole world lieth in wickedness."

"Jesus."

"Yeah. Sort of. How many kids?"

"Thought I saw two."

"Girls or boys?"

"Don't know." Casper bent down for a better look at his fender. "Oh yeah," he said. "The whole world. I see it now."

"'We know that we are of God,'" I told Casper, "'and the whole world lieth in wickedness.' First Epistle of John."

Casper wasn't much interested in the context. The road atlas was his good book. "I better get a rag," he said, but I stopped him and called Ruiz after all.

Flynn and his chirpy colleague came too well after the sun was up, and they took their samples and snapped their photos and then finally gave Casper leave to clean his quarter panel. The writing, of course, was all dry by then and didn't much want to wash off, so Casper brought out his compound and his buffer. He'd put on a bathrobe but hadn't cinched it shut.

"What is it with men around here and underpants?" Ruiz asked me.

I couldn't begin to say. I wore ordinary Jockeys but only ever under stuff.

"Why do you think they keep coming here?" I asked her.

"Don't know," she said and glanced towards Ronnie's. "Where's he?"

"Had an engagement," is how I put it.

"Out stealing something?"

"Ronnie and Queenie kind of hit it off."

"My Queenie?"

I nodded.

"What was he even doing over there?"

Ruiz somehow pieced it all together from just my hangdog look. She sighed a couple of times and sat down on the curb.

"Y'all ruin everything," she said.

Then I saw Ronnie coming from the top of the road on foot with his loud, green suit coat slung over his shoulder. He was untucked and looked like a man who'd been hoofing it for a while.

"Called you a hundred times," he shouted my way.

I waited on him to walk on up. "Phone's in the house," I said.

"Queenie?" Ruiz had gotten to her feet by then. She didn't say it like she was hoping for an answer but more like she'd prefer a contradiction out of Ronnie.

"Says she don't do rides," was Ronnie's response, and he invited us to be incredulous with him since almost all of Ronnie's getting around was based on people doing rides.

Ruiz went with, "Queenie!?" another time and then shook her head and stepped over to watch Casper buff his camper van.

It got left to me to tell Ronnie about the paint that had been on it.

"We need to get on this thing," Ronnie told me and then sniffed his suit coat. "Going to put this in the dryer. Smells like sex and stuff, you know?"

"You didn't take it off?"

"Tried to," Ronnie said. He was on his way to my house by then because he didn't own a dryer. He called back to me as he went, "but she's the sort that runs everything."

I heard Ruiz mutter, "Queenie," one time more from over by Casper's van.

On our way out to the western edge of the county, Ronnie described his night with Queenie, which came across as a strenuous ordeal.

"Bossy, that one," was kind of the boileddown version. "I launched her into orbit. You can be sure of that, but damned if she didn't talk me through it all."

"I'm kind of grateful for Bossy," I confessed to him. "Otherwise I'd just be wandering around."

"She had all the same stuff," Ronnie informed me. "Only, you know, browner."

"Yeah, figures." By then I was proud of not having said "Teeny" even once.

It was a bit of a chore to find Doodle's house because we'd both forgotten his actual name, and Ronnie couldn't get Sugar on the phone. So we stopped and asked whoever we saw and finally ran up on an old country coot who was hanging around at his mailbox.

I thought maybe he was looking for a government check or waiting for a ride, but when Ronnie asked him what he was up to, he told us, "Thinking I'll paint it." He didn't, of course, have a brush or any paint.

He'd known Doodle well, but they'd fallen out. He couldn't remember why.

"Used to see him go by, but then he got sick. That's what people said anyway."

"Had a stroke, we hear," I told him.

"Then he went missing," Ronnie said.

"Might have just died. People'll do that."

We allowed that was a possibility but still wanted to have a look, so he provided us the customary brand of country directions that had us turning at various spots where stuff only used to be. I left Ronnie to guide us over to what had passed with Doodle for a homestead, which looked to be a salvage yard with a shack in the middle of it.

The place wasn't abandoned exactly because we pulled up to find a couple of boys helping themselves to a tractor transmission. They watched us roll in and watched especially Ronnie climb out of the car. His green suit had a way of being interesting.

"Hey here," Ronnie said and told them what our business was.

They had that transmission dangling on a hoist and never stopped easing it towards their truck bed. They didn't appear to care if we decided they were helping themselves to the thing. That's a regular feature of rural thievery. You go around doing what you want to do and dare somebody to stop you.

One of those boys had a chaw in his cheek about the size of a baby's fist, and naturally, he was the one who did all the talking.

"Doodle done gone off," was what I decided he told us. "Been, hell, three weeks?"

His buddy nodded and then said, "Four."

"Where to?" Ronnie asked.

That wasn't a matter that interested them at all, and by their expressions, you'd have thought Ronnie had requested something algebraic.

"We're going to poke around," Ronnie told those boys.

The one with the tobacco shrugged and spat.

The house wasn't locked. The front door wasn't even shut, and there were two hens on the sofa and a vacant spot along the wall where I had to figure Doodle had probably kept his massive TV.

A bucket of potatoes was rotting in the kitchen, and crusty pots and dishes were piled up in the sink. The bed sheets were gray but had likely started ivory, and I left Ronnie to check out the bathroom. I didn't have the steel for that.

Ronnie pointed out the medicine bottles on the end table next to one of the chickens. There were eight or ten of them, the orange plastic kind.

"I'm guessing," Ronnie told me in his Sherlocking voice, "old Doodle wasn't fit to go too far."

So we looked, or we went out back anyway and stuck our heads in a couple of sheds along with one container box that Doodle had probably pulled off a train somewhere. More rusting junk, but no sign of him, and we walked out to where the yard stopped at a field planted with about the rattiest soybeans I've ever seen. They were spindly and looked about half burned up from too much sun and too little water, and there was a stand of yellow pines across the way that bean field wrapped around.

"Might as well look," Ronnie said, and that was the fundamental difference between Sherlocking Ronnie and regular Ronnie. Regular Ronnie had precious little in the way of routine initiative, so there was rarely a thing in this life he'd believe he might as well just do.

"I'll bet he wandered off," I told him on the way and was reminded of my Great Aunt Pearl who came to be demented, and when she'd go roaming, people would bring her home until one day nobody did.

"Some boy found her on a coon hunt," I informed Ronnie. "She was all bones and dentures by then."

Those pine trees were growing around a pond that explained the state of the field since there was more mud in it than water, and the pump they'd irrigated with was sitting on a mound of clay and not even damp. Other than that, the place was trashed up with beer cans, gas jugs, and fertilizer bags. Worse, it was buggy with mosquitoes and gnats and some kind of biting fly, so I was satisfied after a glance around, but Sherlocking Ronnie was all about due diligence. He ignored the bugs, rolled up his trousers, and embarked on a regular tour.

Ordinarily, I would have struck out along with him, but the bugs were bad and the mud was worse, so this time I stayed put and was just about to slip back into the field when Ronnie told me, "Simpson."

He was nearly in the middle of that muck hole, right on the edge of what was left of the water, and he was pointing down in the direction of the slop.

I couldn't see anything special. "What is it?"

Ronnie picked up a stick and poked around before he told me, "Feet."

13

They needed a tow truck to haul Doodle out because the muck didn't want to turn loose, and at first Grimes and the tow-truck driver wouldn't hear any advice from Ronnie. Grimes even strung up a length of yellow tape and tried to make Ronnie stand behind it, but Ronnie had been the one to find the man and wouldn't be neglected or shoved aside.

Ruiz had to serve as the grown up. That was probably what wearied her most. It was hard enough to chase around after a Satanic homicidal crew without needing as well to bother herself with every upset and squabble. Grimes was a bad one in the general course of things for getting and staying peeved. Throw in Ronnie, and everything grew worse.

"Sweet creeping Christ!" is what Ruiz decided to tell them both. It probably didn't hurt that she showed Grimes and Ronnie her gun.

They got along after that by detesting each other in relative silence. Grimes still grunted whenever Ronnie crowded close, and Ronnie made his usual Sherlocking noises.

The tow truck driver finally managed to snatch our corpse out of the mud. He did it slowly with a loop of chain, but the body still made an awful racket. Fortunately, it came out of the slop in just one piece. We couldn't know exactly who it was but assumed it was probably Doodle, and because there was water standing where he'd been stuck, we couldn't tell much about his hole at all.

Ronnie had found a couple of stacks of stones in the vicinity, but neither was as ambitious as the one we'd come across in the woods. We'd looked in the trees for creepy rube art and had cast around for maybe a morsel of Scripture left for us in blood, but aside from the rocks and very possibly Doodle, we'd not turned up anything.

Ruiz, naturally, had to scour the area for herself, and she got Grimes and a uniformed cop and Flynn's chirpy colleague to help her, but they didn't manage to come up with stuff on their own.

"So what do we think?" Ruiz asked Flynn once he had the body on a tarp and had rinsed it off a bit.

"We think he's past saving."

That was the circle of life with those folks. Grimes was hard on civilians. Ruiz was hard on Grimes. And Flynn was quite pleased to be as hard as he liked on Ruiz.

"Find anything in the house?" Ruiz asked, finally turning to me and Ronnie.

"A couple of chickens," Ronnie told her. "A bucket of

rotten potatoes."

"Serpent of old?" she wanted to know.

Me and Ronnie shook our heads.

With dead Tito and all that mess in the woods, stuff had been rounding up for me into something peculiar and Godawful, but it hardly felt special being with Doodle out in that fly-blown bog.

Early on I'd been thinking that devil crew was keen on something in a way I'd never be, that they'd taken a thread of the Bible and had bent it around to suit them, which meant they might have been altogether nuts but in a faithful, organized way. I suspected there was purpose behind what they got up to and some sort of guiding belief, but the more I saw, the less I felt that way.

They'd killed three men and stuck them in holes, had buried a live one under home goods, and maybe those guys were all scoundrels who'd earned exactly what they got, but I couldn't say that for certain. Ruiz hadn't established it yet. We had Scripture to give us a baseline and stacks of rocks and twig art to make it all seem kind of churchly in the wild, but the longer I stayed around it all, the more the nastiness came through.

If anything, it felt worse with Doodle, partly because nobody had found him for so long. Who was to say, before me and Ronnie, if anybody had even looked. And he was sick and failing already, so there wasn't much cause to speed him on.

Ruiz had already collected information on the man. She didn't bother to ride around like we did, but she found out what she needed, and once I'd mentioned Doodle to her, she'd troubled herself to look him up.

"Killed his wife," she told us as we stood there eyeing the body. "Hit her with a camp ax is what they think, but she didn't die right away. Stayed addled for a year or two and then hemorrhaged and kicked off. Then he married her sister," Ruiz informed us. "She just disappeared. They still don't know what happened to her."

She had me and Ronnie walk her up to the house since we'd been inside already and could tell her what we'd touched.

Along the way we explained there were hens on the sofa, and that was the cleanest part of the place.

"No Bible stuff?" she wanted to know.

"Uh-uh," I said, "but maybe the worst sheets I've ever seen."

One of the hens had gone off on an errand or something, and the other one was happily perched on a sofa pillow that had a needlepoint man on it with a needlepoint fishing rod.

Ruiz parked herself in the middle of the room, which I'd noticed she tended to do, and then she slowly turned and had a careful, gradual look all over. There was quite a lot to see in Doodle' s parlor because filth and neglect have a way of creeping and fouling everything, so there was trash on the floor and fuzzy mildew on the ceiling and a full range of squalid details in between.

"What's that smell?" Ruiz asked.

"Feet and stuff." That from Ronnie who still appeared to feel at least mildly inclined to stand up for Doodle a bit. "Man had a stroke," Ronnie reminded us. "It's not like he could get around and clean."

I couldn't imagine even a fit and well Doodle had been much of a housekeeper judging from the antique levels of trashy living I could see, but I didn't quarrel with Ronnie about it, left that sort of thing to Ruiz.

"If he hadn't killed his wives," she volunteered, "one of them might have run the sweeper."

It was worse the second time somehow. The first time through, that house had been impressively, even jarringly nasty, but going slowly from room to room with Ruiz meant more exposure to the particulars, the hairballs and the shrouds of dust and the socks everywhere and the food. Most especially the stink which ebbed and flowed depending on where you were.

"Could be they didn't even come in here," Ronnie suggested to us. "Maybe there are some things the devil can't make you do."

"Door was open?" Ruiz asked us.

And I was nodding and giving Ruiz some sense of where we'd walked and what we'd seen when Ronnie jerked open a closet door right there in the brief hallway and said, "Hell," and then called us over by telling us, "Y'all."

"Give place unto wrath." It was neat again, carefully written across the top door rail with a finger. Almost fancy, like with "Serpent of Old" and done in the same russet red.

Ruiz had barely looked my way before I told her, "Romans, twelve or thirteen maybe. 'Avenge not yourselves, but give place unto wrath. For it is written, vengeance is mine, saith the Lord.'"

Ruiz pulled out her phone and took a couple of snapshots. "Give place unto wrath?" she asked me.

"I always thought it meant, you know, don't kill folks with bricks. Choke it all back. Tamp it down," I told her.

"So...what? They're getting the Bible wrong?"

"We wouldn't have fifty kinds of churches if people didn't do that."

I stayed in the shower that evening long enough for my water to go tepid, and even still I didn't feel all that clean. The crew in paper suits were kind of shielded from the squalor, but I came home wanting to burn my clothes and throw away my shoes. Instead, I just put them on the back porch with plans to touch them in about a week.

Ruiz didn't drop by. I'd thought she might if only for me to serve as a backstop for whatever she'd come up with. Ronnie, on the other hand, let himself in without going to the trouble of knocking, and I figured he wanted to toss his green suit into my washing machine.

That wasn't it though. Ronnie hadn't even changed but seemed content to go on wearing clothes that had been in Doodle' s house. He flopped right down in my best chair, my only chair actually, so I had to do the strategic work of lowering myself to the futon, which had been advertised to me as a cheap sofa you could sleep on, but it was too short for sleeping and too low for sitting. It was mostly just a cushion on the floor.

"Don't know what to tell Sugar," was how Ronnie started.

"About what?"

"You know. Queenie." Ronnie drew a deep breath and let it all out in the sort of sigh that fit a man lounging around morosely in a loud green suit.

"What about her?"

"I'm thinking Queenie might be it for me."

I was aware immediately that I didn't want to know what that meant, but it wasn't like I could hope to dodge the news just by being noncommittal.

"Right," was what I went with, and then I hunkered on the futon and waited.

"Thought for sure it'd be a one-time thing, you know? I was about half loaded, and she was in the mood for beef."

I failed to say, "Teeny beef." I don't quite know how.

"Have you talked to her since?"

"Don't need to," Ronnie told me. "Sometimes you know what you know."

That wasn't quite true. You always know what you know, but you can't be sure in every instance that what you know is worth knowing.

"Talk to Queenie," I suggested and shared with Ronnie a brief story about a girl I'd been convinced was powerfully attracted to me when it turned out I pretty much repulsed her.

"Yeah, well," Ronnie said, "that's you."

"Why would Sugar care anyway?"

Ronnie snorted at the foolishness of such a question, shook his head, couldn't even see fit to respond.

"I'm pretty sure she's a prostitute." I hated to give Ronnie the hard news, but he appeared to be half begging for it.

Ronnie took it well enough. "Yeah," he told me, "sometimes."

"Like when she's having, you know, sex," I said, "with people like you."

"Naw. We've got an understanding, me and Sugar."

Sitting there listening to Ronnie functioned as a lesson for me in our human capacity to explain the world to ourselves on generous terms. Ronnie was never going to be disappointed or, in any meaningful sense, proved wrong because he selected what he felt pulled to believe and chucked everything else aside. I couldn't imagine Queenie had given him a second thought beyond muttering over the mess he'd probably made wherever she lived, but Ronnie knew at his sentimental core that she was pining for him, and he wanted to know how to tell his hooker girlfriend who most certainly wouldn't care.

We're all living fiction to some degree. Me with Ruiz, for whom I was merely hardware, but I stayed convinced that she'd think better of me in due time. Janet and Casper who kept riding the roads in an ever larger camper van as if there was something worthwhile between here and Omaha, and Becky who kept tinkering with the Double D menu in hopes, I guess, of coming up with an entree that would finally make the place a going concern. Triumph lay ahead for us all, just slightly past the horizon.

That crew of mankillers probably wasn't much different. I suspected they'd decided there'd one day be an end of murdering men, sticking them in holes and piling up fieldstones, killing bobcats for their blood.

People need to believe satisfaction and enlightenment are yet to come. Who can blame us? I often did what Ronnie was doing but ordinarily not out loud, so I wasn't hard bent to blow holes in his thinking. I didn't know Queenie well enough to be dead certain he wasn't right, though I was sufficiently acquainted with Sugar to advise Ronnie, "Hell, just tell her."

So he borrowed my phone, dialed her up, and said, "Sugar, hey. We're through."

I don't know where she was or exactly what he'd caught her doing, but Sugar took the news poorly and at full volume. I could hear her yelling.

"See?" Ronnie told me and then thanked me in a sarcastic way and went home.

Rochelle was in a sour mood by the time I got to work in the morning, and he was the sort who wouldn't tell you why until well after you no longer cared. He was pouting when I rolled in and claimed the stew pots were all greasy and I hadn't scraped the griddle down the way that he preferred.

I said, "All right," like I usually did and made out to feel instructed since there was no point in biting back at Rochelle when he'd decided to mope and fume.

He even snapped at Becky once she'd asked him about an order of toast through the service window, and then Rochelle snatched off his apron and threw it on the floor. He marched straight out the back door. Becky came through and left behind him.

She called out, "Ro!" a couple of times as she tried to chase him down.

I was reminded of the morning I'd happened onto them in the walk-in freezer when they'd worked to leave me with the impression they were up to nothing at all.

They had a lively conversation between the dumpster

and the wash pails, and I could see a bit of it through the doorway if I milled around just so. Rochelle was agitated and sharply unhappy about something while Becky, of all people, was working to soothe him and calm him down.

She normally served as an instigator and an all-purpose belittler of humans, and I would have been doubtful the woman had a consoling bone in her body until I saw her with my own eyes lay a soothing hand to Rochelle and tell him something that didn't look like one of her usual, snarky instructions.

Then Ivy, who wore a hair net and a pink waitress' uniform and had worked at Double D's for going on three decades, wondered at me through the service window what the hell the hold up was. I heard her anyway but could see just her waitress' tiara. Ivy was that tiny and shrunken. So I stayed busy with the griddle and the fryer and was still at it by the time Becky and Rochelle came back in.

Becky went through to the front. Rochelle put on his apron. I gave him the time to tell me whatever he felt might work.

"I'm going through something," he eventually said.

"Want to talk about it?" I asked him.

"Thought I just did."

Then Rochelle greased the hot top precisely the way he liked it and scraped all my crusty rubbish away.

My working theory had Rochelle sexually conflicted between his boyfriend and our boss Becky, two categorically different things. So it was far tougher than Ronnie's trouble choosing between a white girl and a black one, and I figured Rochelle was torn in a substantial way. I had a rooting interest, of course, and was pulling for the boyfriend since I couldn't bring myself to wish Becky on a guy.

Consequently, it proved to be a fine morning to talk about dead Doodle since, as topics went, it was part homicidal, part home economics, along with a little theology as well.

"What did he do, this Doodle?" Rochelle asked because he'd decided this world was obliged to be just and righteous, notwithstanding all the evidence that ran the other way.

"Sort of killed his wife. Then married her sister. Could be he killed her too."

"And he was loose?"

"His word against theirs, you know, and they weren't doing much talking."

Like I'd figured he might, Rochelle hit me with Scripture. "Recompense to no man," he said, "evil for evil."

It was a good day for me to air out to Rochelle the various avenues I'd been traveling because my mess served as a distraction for him and kept me away from his delicate business. We talked about the dead guys and got sidetracked onto Satan before, eventually, I steered things in Queenie's direction.

"Ronnie thinks she's the one."

"Queenie?"

I nodded.

"Something go on between them?"

I explained how I'd carried him out to the bar and he hadn't left with me.

"Some other boy fell through for her is what I'd guess." Then Rochelle told me in detail how Queenie organized her sex life. She sounded like Ruiz. She knew what she wanted and got it whenever she liked.

"He's got the wrong end of the stick on this," is what Rochelle finally told me.

"Figured. Should I tell him?"

Rochelle didn't believe so. "She'll do it soon enough." Then he treated me to a couple of verses of *O For A Thousand Tongues To Sing*.

It was one of those days when life goes on. I did my Double D's shift and then drove the activity bus to a ball game out east about thirty miles. They were two innings in when a front came through, washed them out, and back we came. My contractor had nothing for me, so I headed on home for the day and figured I'd probably get waylaid by Ronnie with his latest Queenie news.

Ronnie wasn't on his glider, and I noticed his screen door was standing about half open, which was odd because Ronnie's screen door was often too swollen to move. I called his name from my yard and waited for his usual shout but ended up getting nothing back at all.

I went straight over and could see that Ronnie's front room was in a state. Mail on the floor, an end table turned over, socks all over the place, but that was kind of the natural way of things with Ronnie's domestic situation, so I just stayed where I was and said, "Hey!" a couple of times.

I was aware that occasionally Ronnie would move to his back steps to clip his toenails, so that was a possibility I held out and kept on yelling. The Queenie thing worried me because I feared she wasn't a woman who'd let a man down easy. I could picture Ronnie hunting her up to confess his love face-to-face and Queenie making ruthless short work of him.

I stood in his front room and shouted his name some more.

Still nothing, so I milled around in his stuff and clutter. Ronnie had something approaching Doodle decor. No chickens yet and far less mildew, but he probably just needed time.

His TV was on with the sound turned down, and it was tuned to the news from Richmond where a puffy guy in a blazer was making chat with a toothy weather woman in less skirt than she probably needed.

"Ronnie!" I shouted it with enough volume to reach

the backyard for sure.

Still nothing, so I eased down Ronnie's hallway, checking the rooms on either side. The doors were all open except for the bathroom, so pushed on in. It was a dirty towel and soap scum paradise in there.

Ronnie had made a path through his bedroom so he could easily reach his closet and his mattress on the floor. His guest room was littered with grocery sacks and had most of a go-cart in it, which somebody somewhere hadn't (I guess) been caring for quite enough.

The end of the hall gave onto the kitchen, and I could see the plates and mail and mess piled up on Ronnie's dinette. I heard the water in the sink dripping against a saucepan before I'd cleared the corner and could see the cabinet doors. Most of them were standing open, or at the very least cocked ajar, except for the two up over the range hood. They were shut and talking to me.

Russet again and step-van penmanship. "For all have sinned and come short of the glory of God."

14

Ruiz's phone kept going to voicemail, and after I'd left the third urgent message, I decided I probably owed Ronnie something more than just phone calls, so I went to the bottom drawer of my dresser, shifted my too-small trousers aside, and pulled out my great-granddaddy's Colt Peacemaker. There was only one place that I truly felt pulled to go.

I'll admit I didn't rush in past that pipe gate right away but put in another call to Ruiz and left her another message and then shouted for Ronnie while I screwed up the nerve to go onto that farm. That took maybe a quarter hour because I'm not even marginally brave and have a thing about forests and a thing as well about getting shoved into a hole in the ground.

So I was reluctant but finally said, "Well, hell," stuck my gun in my pants and pressed on.

I started with those ruined barns and had another look in the farmhouse, even discovered nerve enough for a poke through the work shed once I'd finally gotten the hammer of my old Peacemaker drawn and cocked.

I tried Ruiz another couple of times, had to work to

get a signal for it, and I managed to tell her voicemail where I was and where I'd be going. I wondered if she'd realize what a catch I'd been once she came across me dead.

Then I headed on up the hillside, went through the pecan grove and across to the spine of the pasture from where I could see dead Tito's pond bank, but mercifully there was no sign of Ronnie down there. So I glanced up towards the treeline and then climbed to the edge of the woods.

It was getting dusky by then, and I finally managed to raise Ruiz on the phone. She hadn't heard any of my messages and started in on how she'd been chasing after one lead or another.

I had to horn in to tell her, "They grabbed Ronnie."

"Who?"

"'For all have sinned and come short of the glory of God.' It was on his kitchen cabinets."

"Where are you?"

I told her.

"Just wait. I'm coming."

"Got to help him," I said in my best tortured way, and I imagined the anguish she might feel once she was cradling my lifeless body. It stirred and excited me to think of it because I'm an idiot, I guess.

"Wait!" she said.

But I played it like I was living out my days in a potboiler, and I believe I even told Ruiz, "Didn't we have some fun." Then I killed the call and took a half dozen steps into the actual forest where I had the good sense to stop and wonder what the hell I was even about.

Pausing to think all my options through impressed me as a sensible tactic, but I'd gone and blustered already, so I had to go into the woods. I took time to check my Colt. It was a single-action revolver, so you had to cock it every time you fired. The thing was good for a duel and heavy enough to serve in a pinch as a hammer but probably not the ideal weapon for meeting Satan's minions with.

"This isn't good," I told myself. It had become kind of a mantra for me. Then my phone went off, and that also wasn't so swell.

Ruiz had concluded, in the intervening moments, that I was some species of moron, and she informed me of it colorful language. I could tell she was in her Ford.

"Twenty minutes. Sit tight," she told me.

I think I said back that I would and then shut off my phone and went deeper into the woods.

I realized immediately I liked the forest far less in the dusk than the daylight, and once I'd ventured well in among the oaks and poplars, I had to stop to let my eyes adjust. I also listened out for unwoodsy racket but only heard a deer (I had to hope) snorting and a mockingbird chirping away. I could see decently enough after a couple of minutes and so continued another twenty yards or so until a thump from somewhere up ahead caused me to pull up short. I stood still and waited. Breeze in the treetops. More birdcall. Little else.

It went like that for longer than I'd care to admit—a couple of steps, a lot of stopping—and I recognized at the time that I was sort of waiting for Ruiz by advancing into the forest hardly at all. That allowed me to make a show of being courageous and intrepid while not, in fact, being either one awfully much.

By then, I was scared for me considerably more than I was scared for Ronnie. I did hope if they beat him, they'd use a big brick and wouldn't make it last. Then I caught myself wondering how exactly Ronnie had earned their attention. Was it possible he'd been a violent lout and a deviant like the rest? He'd owned up to some of that, but maybe he'd hedged and it was worse.

Then I heard something that wasn't a deer and wasn't a mockingbird either and was instead a woman talking, saying, "That he may sift you as wheat." She said something else that also sounded like Scripture. I couldn't hear that part clearly, but I could tell well enough that she was getting closer with every word she spoke.

I don't know how I failed to turn and run. I certainly thought about it, and I even imagined myself pursued by a pack of banshee women and fixed for a moment on that sweet taste that comes when you get knocked hard in the head.

Maybe because it didn't think of it as outright flight and it seemed better than being a coward, I hustled over to a bushy cedar tree and climbed straight up into the thing. It was a monster for a cedar, and I went as high as I could go, was well up in the crown when I lost my grip on great grandaddy's gun, and it bounced off a couple of limbs and dropped to the ground. Not onto leaf litter, of course, but straight onto a clump of rocks, and since the thing was cocked and ready, it went off like a howitzer might.

I got as small and still as possible up in the top of that cedar, and soon enough I could see them coming my way. They were carrying lanterns, the old kerosene kind, so what light they had was dim and yellow and feeble.

I couldn't tell how many there might be. It seemed like maybe a half dozen, and one of them stood for a moment right next to the trunk of the tree I was in. She picked up my pistol, eyed the landscape around while I held my breath and puckered and prayed she wouldn't decide to look up.

She had braids coiled on top of her head and was wearing one of those long flowery dresses like women used to go around the prairie in. Another one wandered into view, and she was dressed just the same. Her I didn't recognize, but I'd seen enough pictures of hair-braid lady to know her for Iphigenia Mona Duncan Orestes in the flesh.

She said something to all the other ones, and that gang went off at a trot.

I started to climb down but changed my mind because I remembered that crew was wily, and I feared they might be laying for me not so far off in the dark. So down I'd go, and they'd have me and Ronnie, and soon enough we'd just be four legs sticking up out of the muck.

The flies were biting, and the ants were crawling on me, and a squirrel came up briefly for a look. I thought about turning my phone on just to use the light, but I knew it would chirp and beep and warble and very possibly give me away. So I just sat and felt sorry for myself and wondered what that bunch was doing to Ronnie.

Soon enough, I had to pee of course, so there was that strategy to think on, and I kept hearing noises out in the dark that I decided sounded like bears. So I was having an unhappy stretch high in my cedar in the forest, when I saw something coming my way brighter than kerosene lantern light. I figured they'd gone to get something modern to return and find me with, so I pressed against the trunk and breathed hardly any at all.

The beam kept circling my way, kept making orderly loops, and as I tried to ease higher in the canopy, I missed a branch and yelped. It was enough to give me away, and that light soon found me in my treetop. I clenched and waited for a fortyfive slug to do what it would do.

Then the beam shifted and played along the ground, and I caught a glimpse of some homely shoes.

"Hey," Ruiz said. "You want the light or not?"

It proved easier on my dignity to climb down in the dark.

"What put you up there?" she wanted to know.

"I saw them. Some of them anyway. It's women all right."

"See your neighbor?"

"No," I said and then told her because I felt like I had to, "Those ladies kind of got my gun."

"Where'd they go?"

"Came from there?" I pointed. "Went out down that way."

"How many?"

"I'd say six or seven. Carrying old kerosene lanterns. Had on dresses like you'd see on a wagon train. Where's Grimes and them?" I asked her.

She shook her head and left me. I could follow along or not.

I kept crowding Ruiz more than she could stand. She headed deeper into the woods instead of out.

When I asked her why, she said, "Just looking." She told me I could stay put if I liked.

They'd restacked rocks, maybe in the same places. Because it was dark, I was too turned around to tell. But there were field stones piled up like before, and we found the embers from a campfire that were still hot and glowing, but I had to admit those ladies had policed the area well. There was nothing to see except rocks and firewood and some kind of half-assed rube art Ruiz found hanging from a limb. It was made from sticks and strings and feathers and moss and was dangling by a length of vine.

Ruiz was all business out there. She did what she did the way she saw fit, and I could trail along behind her or stay parked back in the dark. My leading fear was that the crew would come back with five rounds left in my Colt, but along with that, I was worried about finding Ronnie's battered body either stuck in a hole or laid out in some creepy, Satanic way.

Ruiz, for her part, just forged ahead playing her beam all around. She failed to keep her free hand on her gun, which is what I would have suggested because of how quietly women in prairie dresses can move through the woods at night.

She eventually spied some kind of lean-to, a thing like frontiersmen might have built. It had been put together with branches and limbs, vine bindings and gravity. It was maybe four feet tall and twice that long, and there was no door on our end, so Ruiz circled around with me following tight behind her.

I let her look inside alone because I'm a squeamish coward, and she didn't give me much of a sign since all Ruiz said was, "Huh." Then she hunted up a poking stick and jabbed at something I couldn't see.

"Is it him?"

She didn't say yes or no but instead grabbed me and pulled me her way so I could see for myself a dead bob-cat and a pair of dead raccoons. They'd been bled and gutted a while back and were laid out on a bed of twigs in a semi-artful way.

Ruiz swept the woods ahead of us with the beam of her light, and I near about had a stroke when she caught the eyes of a doe.

She took pity on me and finally said, "Come on."

Once we were clear of the scrub and back into the pasture, I all but begged her to call for help.

"I'm getting to it," she told me and pulled out her phone.

I heard the call go through. She'd gone straight to the boss who must have insisted on it. They did have bodies piling up, and when your people are getting murdered in a colorful, disturbing way, it hardly matters what sort of trash they were.

"Yes, sir," Ruiz said three or four times and then signed off and asked me, "Happy?"

It wasn't like Ruiz was the sort who could sit around

and wait for reinforcements. She had grounds to search and structures to clear, and we started out by heading down towards the pond where they'd planted Tito.

"You don't have an extra gun, do you?" I asked her along the way.

"Yeah," she said but never broke her stride.

That pond bank looked in no way freshly trod upon. Tito's hole was filling itself in from weather and erosion, and what forensic trash hadn't blown clear had gotten fouled with mud.

Then we went and checked the barns and the tool shed and the farmhouse, but they were exactly like we'd left them. Nothing appeared to have changed at all.

"Ideas?" Ruiz said.

I had one, sort of. It seemed to me, even if you were actively in league with Satan, you were probably going to want a few animal comforts like a roof and a flushing toilet, maybe even electric lights to come home to after a hard day of pulverizing folks.

"Can't camp in those dresses," is mostly what I ended up telling Ruiz.

"Where then?" she asked me.

"Whelan place." I pointed, not necessarily in the right direction but off somewhere in the dark. "It's right next to here," I told her.

She had her phone out by then and was checking her map like you do anymore.

Our route carried us wide of one of the barns and directly past the tool shed where we picked up a path that looked like something a couple of deer had made. It was six inches wide and meandering until we hit a hedgerow where it turned into a regular thoroughfare with stacked rocks and little hanging twig cages by way of decoration.

We had to skirt a fallow bean field to reach any of the buildings, but we could see well enough that the old farmhouse was lit up.

"Help's coming," I reminded her.

"Let's see what we see," she said and kept going.

We could hear them as we closed and see them once we'd circled around to where we had a view of the front yard of that old house. It was in a grove of ancient, gnarly white oaks, and that crew had gathered on the lawn. They were kneeling on the ground, had their arms stretched out in front of them and were praying or chanting or something. I couldn't hear what they were saying from over where we were.

Ruiz wouldn't stop, kept easing closer, and I stuck tight with her, lacked the nerve to do anything else.

"Go back?" I said.

Ruiz clearly didn't want to, but she had a job and a boss and some marginal sense of proper, responsible duty, and she was about to retreat my way when we both heard Ronnie speak up.

He was over there among them, and Ronnie started giving reasons why he wasn't a fellow worth killing.

"Ain't nobody anywhere," Ronnie declared, "treats women better than me. Check around. You'll see."

He didn't sound rattled at all. Ronnie had long had a knack of talking his way out of almost anything.

"Y'all are all sensible girls. Level-headed. Particular, I can see that, so I know you'll ask around before you do something you can't undo. That's fair, isn't it? Don't seem like much."

That crew just kept on saying their stuff, speaking their spell or whatever it was while Ronnie kept working to prattle himself free.

"I guess that tears it," Ruiz said and not in a low, private way just for me. Then she pulled out her pistol, shouted, "Hey!" and fired two rounds in the air. That seemed rash to me, and I believe I even said as much.

The effect on those women was curious to see. They looked our way, got up off their knees, and then scattered, but not in a panic. More like a yoga class breaking up after the hour is done. They went off in various directions and emptied out the yard. Left Ronnie alone, and we could finally see him by then. He was parked on a chair and tied to it, didn't appear to be wearing a thing.

Ruiz was careful and professional as she closed upon the house, notwithstanding what Ronnie was saying from over by the tree.

"Gone. Lit out. Tore down through the woods."

"Shut up," Ruiz finally requested.

He even almost did, but first he had to tell us, "Wait'll Queenie hears about this."

Ruiz went in the farmhouse and came back out before she bothered to mess with Ronnie. He was naked all right and had stuff painted on him in bobcat/human/raccoon blood, I had to think. There were letters and symbols and a picture or two. Somebody had gone to the bother to even paint what looked like barber-pole stripes on little Ronnie.

I imagined they'd only loaded the brush the once.

15

Ruiz refused to leave the property in fear those devil girls would come back and make off with evidence she'd be needing, but she insisted me and Ronnie go out and meet boss Cliff and them, which Ronnie allowed he'd be happier doing if he could locate a pair of trousers.

Until then, Ronnie had seemed pleased to strut around in the altogether and didn't appear to mind at all when Ruiz drew him into the light so she could see the stuff that was painted on him.

Across his back, they'd written *And I saw a great white throne* along with a few additional scraps from Revelation that were more in the way of the famous bits like *And night will be no more* and *Behold, I am making all things new*, along with *I am the alpha and omega*. There was a sun on Ronnie's back and a crescent moon on his chest, and a tree with an apple on it down around Ronnie's belly, which had the effect of making little Ronnie a striped snake in the garden.

"Maybe," Ruiz allowed, "when it grows up."

Ronnie couldn't find any pants but did grab a dish

towel off the clothesline, and Ruiz told him before I could that it would surely be more than enough.

"Go on. I'm good," Ruiz said, and I led Ronnie around the field and down the path we'd come in on with my phone to light the way.

"About had them talked out of it," Ronnie assured me.

"Didn't look that way."

"They were coming around."

That was Ronnie all over. He believed he could get out of just about anything, especially if there were females involved because Ronnie put a lot of stock in the potency of his charm and persuasion.

"That Tamara girl's in with them. She's all right," Ronnie said. "Lady in charge was half sweet on me."

"The one with the braids?" I asked him.

Ronnie nodded. "Iphy," he called her. "She drew this right here." Ronnie pointed towards a stick man on his shoulder.

"She took my gun."

"Saw it. They said you were shooting at them."

"I dropped it. I was up in a cedar tree."

Ronnie gave that some thought and nodded liked that was where he'd expected I'd be.

"They tell you what they were up to?" I asked him.

"Spouted a lot of Bible stuff, or something."

"They say anything about Doodle or Tito?"

Ronnie shook his head. "Two of them thought I was some guy named Paul, but another one straightened them out. They went on for a pretty good while about our truck."

"Your truck. What about it?"

"It was like this." Ronnie joined his hands with his fingers intertwined. "They said once we showed up here and took it, their stuff all came together. The way I heard it, they'd been waiting for a sign." Then he went where I'd figured he'd have to go. "Did Queenie ask about me?"

"Hell, I don't know. I've been up in a tree."

"She's bound to be all tore up," he said, and I didn't have the heart to contradict him, given that Ronnie was painted and naked with a dish towel on his junk.

I did say, "I'm done with that rollaway bed."

"Yeah, well," Ronnie told me, "if that's what you want to think."

We were past the work shed by then and approaching that mildewed farmhouse. I could see headlights up ahead right around the pipe gate.

"It's all men, you know?" Ronnie told me. "Or they wouldn't even be here."

I did know. As a man, you want to set yourself apart, but it's hard to be one of us and not stay tuned into the trouble since we have an ugly history of being bigger and stronger and getting (however it suits us) what we want.

By the time we reached the lights up ahead, a whole crew of cops was there, including the big chief Cliff in his pressed uniform and Grimes with some kind of rifle.

"Where's she?" Cliff asked us.

"Watching the house," I told him.

"He all right?" Grimes wanted to know once he'd gotten a look at the state of Ronnie.

Ronnie said, "What does it look like?" and flung his dishtowel aside.

"Somebody painted his pecker," Grimes said and fished a pair of filthy coveralls for Ronnie out of the wheel well of his trunk.

I led Cliff and Grimes and a quartet of SWAT boys back down the track where we'd just come from, and I got pressed to answer stuff I didn't know along the way, like who exactly had been holding Ronnie and how many of them there were, if they were armed and sober and primed for a fight, if they were rational actors at all.

The SWAT bunch wasn't all that impressive. They kept tripping over stuff and had so much gear on that they clattered and rattled all along the way. Those boys weren't going to slip up on anybody. Given the limited call for tactical forces in our little burg, I had to imagine those fellows hardly ever got to suit up and probably didn't get to practice being SWATTY all that much, so their choreography down the track was fairly uninspiring.

They kept looping ahead of each other and squatting, taking aim at nothing much while me and the big boss and Grimes followed along in conversation like we didn't need to worry about where we were going or who we were likely to meet.

"Lesbians or something, aren't they?" That from Grimes, of course.

"I don't think that's it."

Grimes snorted. Boss Cliff, I noticed, snorted a little too.

We all, in the end, select our explanations. Some of us adjust to what's in front of us, but plenty don't and never will. Ronnie wouldn't. He needed to live in a world where women found him irresistible, so that's exactly the world he'd made for himself, and he wouldn't get shouldered out of it. Boss Cliff and Grimes appeared to prefer something else entirely, specifically a spot where women were what they'd decided women ought to be.

"I get the feeling," I said, "some of them have been kind of knocked around."

"Right," is what I heard back from Cliff who nodded like women getting knocked around bordered on unhelpful but was hardly fit cause to pound a guy and stick him in a hole.

"What's all this?" Grimes asked once we were passing through the hedgerow, a thirty-yard band of trees that separated the two farms.

He was looking at stacked rocks and painted tree trunks and twig art hanging from limbs.

"Part of their thing," is what I told him. "They've got, like, a religion."

He had Grimes shine his flashlight beam on a twig cage that caught his eye. It had hair in it and nut hulls along with a few strips of denim.

"Some kind of voodoo?" Cliff asked me.

I flashed on my father in his linty black suit, pouring with sweat, with is Bible raised over his head. "Yeah," I said back, "some kind."

We arrived at the farmhouse to find the SWAT boys shouting orders from the yard. They'd discovered somebody in the building. It happened to be Ruiz, but those fellows weren't really in the distinction business and so were taking turns telling her to get down and come out, depending on which of them was doing the shouting.

Ruiz, for her part, stepped onto the porch and instructed them all to shut up.

"What are we looking at?" Boss Cliff asked, which would have required from Ruiz a fairly involved disquisition, so instead, she just opened the screen door and motioned for Cliff to go on in.

He did and Grimes did too. I got as far as the front porch before two SWAT boys stopped me, so I asked Ruiz, "What's in there?"

"Regular stuff," she said.

That's how it looked from what I could see through the doorway. Ordinary farmhouse furniture with more than a few female touches like flowers in pots on tables and scarves on some of the lampshades to dampen the light.

"Ronnie says they stuck him." I tapped my neck. "Pumped him full of some kind of drug."

Ruiz nodded. "Figures. It's all in there."

She stepped inside long enough to fetch something out, a stack of eight or ten photographs. Some were Polaroids, others printouts, but all of them were pictures of the faces of women who'd been put upon and knocked around. Iphigenia Orestes was among them with her puffy eye and her stitched bottom lip.

Boss Cliff sent SWAT across the landscape to look for those women, but they didn't turn up much at all.

They debriefed Ronnie back at the bank. Me a little too. It fell to Ruiz and Grimes while Flynn and them worked at the farmhouse with those SWAT boys there to clatter and rattle in the yard.

Our end of things started with snapshots of Ronnie. Ruiz enlisted a large, unhappy black woman to handle the camera who let it be known she'd signed on for desk work, answering calls and a little filing, and hadn't wanted or expected to be taking pictures of a naked man all painted up.

Ronnie didn't help much. "My girlfriend's black," he

told her, and thoughts of Queenie (I have to imagine) caused little Ronnie to stir a bit, but Ruiz licked a finger and stuck it in Ronnie's ear, which somehow did the trick, and he deflated.

The reluctant lady with the camera took a bunch of pictures as Ruiz held a ruler next to Ronnie's painted words and stuff.

Upon close inspection underneath a bank of fluorescent lights, we could all see that Ronnie was lavishly illustrated. It looked like they'd drawn all over him before they'd come back to write over him too. Most of it seemed like the work of children or some variation on cave painting. The people were all round heads on sticks, and the landscapes were just horizons with a piece of moon or a sun.

"They talk to you?" Grimes wanted to know.

"A little. Did a lot of praying or something. Singing songs. All of them danced around me some. I do remember that."

"Did they say why you?" Ruiz asked.

Ronnie nodded. "Thought I was Paul."

"Paul who?" Ruiz asked.

Ronnie shrugged.

"Know any Pauls?"

Ronnie said he didn't, but he sort of did, which meant I sort of did too.

"P. C. Blaylock," I told Ruiz. "That's what it says on

the mailbox. We all call him Casper, but his brother or somebody came around once, and he kept calling him Paul."

"Oh, right," Ronnie said.

"What do you know about him?" Ruiz asked us.

"Works on his van a lot," I said.

"Run him," Ruiz told Grimes who went off to bang on a keyboard.

Ronnie scratched at a bit of Proverbs somebody had painted up his thigh—"Fools despise wisdom and instruction"—and he'd wiped out a couple of letters before Ruiz told him, "Stop!"

"Itches like crazy," Ronnie said. "Especially this here." He grabbed little Ronnie and gestured sufficiently to cause the lady with the camera to set it down and go off to file.

Once some lab girl had come by to take samples off of Ronnie, Ruiz escorted him out their back door into some kind of alley where they had a hose that she used to wash him off.

Ronnie wanted me to carry him to the pool hall as soon as they'd cut us loose. He didn't care that he was wearing filthy coveralls and had only gotten about half clean.

"Call her first, huh?" I advised him.

But Ronnie had convinced himself Queenie had been fretting about him, likely to the point of being agonized.

"This thing's got to be face to face," he said and had me drive him straight over. I didn't enter the pool hall until he'd been inside for a minute or two.

I felt like I knew what was going to happen, but I'm routinely wrong about stuff and was hoping I'd go in to find Queenie weeping from relief because Ronnie had been right all along and she was smitten with him. Instead, he was standing at the end of the bar waiting for her to finish with a couple of boys she was pouring tequila shots for.

Rochelle's whiskery friend was parked on his usual stool, and we jerked our heads at each other and then together watched as Ronnie announced to Queenie and the rest of us that he'd been nabbed by a pack of crazy women but everything had turned out all right.

"It was a close run thing there for a while," Ronnie told anybody who cared to hear it, "but I got away before they could do much harm."

Queenie didn't appear to be more interested than the rest of the patrons around, and only I had any idea what Ronnie was actually talking about, so I couldn't much blame the bunch of them for not caring.

When Queenie finally wandered down our way, all she said was, "What'll y'all have?"

Ronnie was crushed, but I could only tell because I'd been around him so long. Crushed Ronnie looks like regular Ronnie, just with some air let out. He couldn't decide if he wanted a drink, so I decided for him.

I shook my head and told Queenie, "He got kidnapped by this bunch, and they pumped him full of some kind of drug. He probably shouldn't be drinking."

Queenie asked Ronnie, "You all right?"

Ronnie merely nodded.

A fellow came over from one of the pool tables with his cue stick and his empty glass. Queenie smacked the bar with her open hand, winked at Ronnie, and went off.

I let Ronnie sleep on my futon that night, and I'll never ask him for a favor from it, never remind him that I put him up and have a thing I need him to do.

He talked a little about Queenie before he dozed off. He talked anyway about women generally, but Queenie is who he meant. It was one of those conversations where I got asked to explain stuff about women, but the point of it all was for me to say I couldn't and not even try to.

Ruiz showed up after midnight and texted me from the porch. When I opened the door, she caught sight of Ronnie sacked out on my sofa.

"Queenie," I said.

That was all Ruiz needed. She left once she'd told me, "Oh."

16

Ronnie was gone by the time I got up for my shift at Double D's. I found him out on his glider smoking and having himself a tallboy for breakfast.

He pointed towards Casper and Janet's place. "We ought to talk to him."

"Let Ruiz and them," I told him back, but I could tell already he wouldn't and that I was likely to find him later fitted out in his loud, green suit.

I couldn't do much about it and decided I wouldn't bother to warn Ruiz because she pretty much knew already what she was up against with Ronnie. So I just went on to work and arrived to find Rochelle in the middle of "Beneath the Cross."

"Saw your buddy last night," I told him.

Rochelle kept singing and squinted at me.

"Cody with the beard."

Rochelle nodded and launched into the refrain.

I let him finish and changed the sink water before I said, "Aren't you two...?"

I made enough of a gesture at Rochelle to prompt him to tell me, "Sometimes."

It had become a "sometimes" world while I wasn't paying strict attention, and I was finding I lacked the proper gearing to be a "sometimes" guy.

"How do you do that?" I asked Rochelle after he'd decided to quit singing. "I'd like to be about half attached to pretty much every damn body."

"What's keeping you?"

I had to think I was built to do one thing at a time, but I couldn't see why that shouldn't be up for adjustment.

"Not sure," I opted to tell Rochelle.

"Try it," he said back and then launched into "Oh, For A Thousand Tongues To Sing" at penetrating volume.

Becky must have heard him in the dining room because she came teetering into the kitchen in what looked like a new pair of strangulating jeans.

I thought she might bark at Rochelle and insist he hold it down, but instead she eased up close beside him, and Rochelle just kept on singing. I scrubbed dishes with a fresh appreciation of what "sometimes" might occasionally mean.

I got called in on a bus route mid-afternoon and then got sent to the lumber yard to pick up a couple of boxes of nails, some deck hangers, and two storm doors, which I carried out to a subdivision on the old Midlothian road that had been a bean field a couple of months back but was known anymore as Magnolia Highlands because the place had been magically transformed into a bean field with houses in it.

I stayed around long enough to pick up the job site with the boss' nephew, Jason, and I told him I was having a rough day trying to figure stuff out. I said I was laboring hard to decide what I thought about retribution and revenge. When was it justified? What were the standards and the obligations, and when did it cross the line and just become an equal wrong?

Jason, of course, was wearing his earbuds and couldn't hear me at all, which I knew going in and counted on and had decided to put to use since I'd found it helped me to talk through stuff I was struggling with out loud.

I drove around a little after I'd left Magnolia Highlands because I wasn't up for any Sherlocking and wanted the sun to set on my day. It just about had by the time I reached my street, but it turned out I'd not stayed away long enough because Casper and Ronnie were brawling out in the middle of our road. Ronnie had on his green suit, and Casper was wearing his chinos and deck shoes, so they came across as white and ungainly and not terribly violent at all.

A few of the other neighbors had gathered around to watch, but they didn't appear to be much interested in the proceedings, probably because Ronnie and Casper were down on the asphalt in a full embrace and were 'fighting' primarily by saying intemperate things to each other.

Casper mentioned the lawyer he intended to call and informed Ronnie he was sleazy trash while Ronnie declared he had fresh info on Casper's violent past that Ronnie said he'd found on his goddamn phone on the goddamn internet. Then I think he bit Casper's ear. That's what it looked like anyway, and Casper surely did raise a shout about it.

I didn't rush straight over to them, couldn't see why it should fall to me to pull apart two grown men even if I was Simpson to Ronnie's Sherlock. So I just let them roll and bicker and took time to greet my neighbors, but then Ronnie started calling for me, so I was about to get involved when Janet came down her driveway and joined us all in the street.

Ronnie, apparently, had told her what to search for on her own goddamn phone, and she'd been studying up on Casper's secret past. He'd had a wife before Janet that she'd not been aware of and a domestic abuse conviction along with a plea to menacing. Restraining orders had been filed against him by a couple of women. If you're up for it and you want to nose around, you can find out anything anymore.

Casper told Janet he was different now. "I was a bad one for drink," he said. "Had all kinds of anger problems, but I got help. You know I'm not like that anymore."

Janet was in a position to vouch for him but had decided she didn't want to. "I need to talk to her, this other wife," Janet said to Casper, which appeared to be about the last thing Casper wanted to hear.

"It was a mistake," he said. "Didn't last any time at all." Then he got peeved in his old way, I have to think, and took it all out on Ronnie who was handy to get punched and pounded and clawed. That's when I went over to kick Casper once and tell him he ought to stop.

A deputy rolled in along about then, but it was only Ike from the middle school picking up some extra hours in his radio car. He didn't even bother to get out but rolled down his window to ask us, "What are y'all doing?"

We looked at each other, those of us upright. One of us had to tell him something, so I got to say, "Aw, you know."

That was good enough for Ike who went on through. Ronnie and Casper were pretty much finished by then since no damage Casper could inflict on Ronnie would even begin to undo what Janet had discovered about his past. So they unclenched and separated, called each other corrosive names, and then Casper followed Janet up their driveway while the rest of us sympathized with Ronnie on the wretched state of his suit.

Ronnie was still filling me in on ugly Casper details when Ruiz rolled up and found us on the glider. Ronnie had stripped out of his suit and was wearing his bath-robe, flannel and filthy, and he opened it up to show Ruiz scrapes he'd gotten in the street. I noticed he'd not yet scoured little Ronnie entirely clean.

"There's your Paul," Ronnie told Ruiz and pointed across the road.

"Yeah." Ruiz apparently had been on her goddamn phone as well. But that wasn't why she'd come. "Need y'all for something." Then she told Ronnie, "Pants."

We both rode in the back of Ruiz's Ford because she had no end of mess up front.

"Found one of them," is all she told us, and then she took a radio call, so we had to sit and wait a while before Ronnie could ask, "Which one? What's she saying?"

"Not a lot."

"Why's that?" Ronnie wanted to know.

Ruiz fished around on her passenger seat and grabbed up an evidence bag. She raised it to where we could see the contents—my great-granddaddy's Colt Peacemaker.

"Suicide looks like," is what Ruiz told us.

I couldn't do anything but sit there and feel sick.

She took us down through a stretch of Whelan ter-ritory I'd never seen before, but there wasn't anything special or different about the Whelan filth and squalor and the stink eye loitering Whelans gave us as we rolled on through.

Back where we ended up, it looked like everybody had quit on agriculture. The fields were all weedy and sunbaked, appeared to have not seen a plow in years. The fences were laid over, and the barns and the houses were coming apart.

"Where is this?" Ronnie wanted to know.

Ruiz pointed towards a treeline. "Place you were," she told him, "is on the other side of that."

Flynn and his girl were out there along with Grimes and a crew of rescue squad boys called, I guessed, to haul the body off.

That lady was in a barn sprawled on the dirt floor. It didn't look like they'd even shifted her yet but just left her where she dropped. Her braided hair was all bloody, and I asked Ruiz, "Can't we look at pictures?"

"Nope," she said. "Didn't bring you out here for that."

She walked both of us in, had us each by an elbow, and she steered us until we were hard beside Iphigenia Mona Duncan Orestes who was a grisly kind of dead. That's what a point-blank .45 will do.

"Recognize this woman?" Ruiz asked us. Ronnie nodded and said, "Iphy."

"How do you know her?"

"I'd say she was the boss of all those girls."

"And you?" Ruiz turned my way.

"She picked up my pistol."

Then Ruiz made us stand there and soak it in before

she told Ronnie, "Burn that suit."

Then she waved the rescue squad boys in who man-
handled the remains.

"Why?" I asked Ruiz once we were back outside and
they were loading Iphigenia Mona Duncan Orestes into
the truck.

"Why what?"

"All of it."

She shrugged.

"Make a guess."

And she only did after she'd waited so long that I'd
decided she wouldn't. "Bully boys are rough and stu-
pid," she told me, "but vengeance kind of is too."

"Where are the rest of them?" Ronnie wanted to
know.

"Around," Ruiz said and had a glance at the tree line.
"We'll scoop them all up in time."

Ronnie tried to sell his story to the Richmond paper
when one of their guys came around, but he disappointed Ronnie with the news that they never paid for what
they printed.

So Ronnie said, "Ok. Five hundred."

That reporter ended up hearing what he needed
from me instead. He came to Double D's, ate early breakfast, late breakfast, and then lunch as well, so I decided
he'd suffered enough and talked to him out back by the
dumpster. His name was Bismarck. I'm sure he had a

first name too, but he was so pleased to be a Bismarck that that's all he'd let you call him. He told me he was a feature writer, and he said that meant he left the hard news to his colleagues while he dug for something better, something usually truer too.

"I'm all who and why," he told me, even reached out and squeezed my shoulder. Bismarck was very likely a decent enough writer but a community-theater-caliber everything else.

I talked to him at length, mostly out at the pool hall. I picked the place because I knew Ronnie wouldn't come in. He was punishing Queenie. He'd tried hot pursuit, but when that didn't work, he snubbed her instead and would send me out to the pool hall so I could casually bring him up just to see what Queenie might say.

Usually it was something on the order of, "Who?"

So I knew I had some safe time to spend with Bismarck at the bar where I let him pay for everything that Queenie decided to bring us, and Ruiz would swing by every now and again to advise me to shut up.

"He'll get it all wrong," was her take, but I knew that didn't matter because I was just indulging that chance to get it all straight in my head. I didn't care what Bismarck wrote, what the people in Richmond printed because I didn't take the *Times-Dispatch* and wouldn't read the story anyway. The way I saw it, I had stuff to figure out and a guy to buy me drinks while I was at it.

So we spent hours in the pool hall eating various bits of pig washed down with Turkey and longnecks while I gave an account of my involvement in a story that started out with big-boned Gail.

I talked a bit about my father, of course, and did it for longer than Bismarck wanted, so I shifted to my mother and talked a bit about her too.

There near the end, Bismarck brought a photographer out with him. She took some pictures of me on the muddy bank of Tito's pond. Then I walked them up through the pasture, through the scrub, and to the treeline where I told them both, "I think I'll stop right here."

A woman in real estate bought Ronnie's house. She went around checking titles, rooting up bargains and the like, and she discovered Ronnie was squatting and paid off the liens and taxes. Then she came over personally to pitch him out because that was the stuff she most enjoyed. That woman ended up on the glider with Ronnie where they had an extended chat, and each of them discovered the other was devious in a beguiling way.

Theirs was a breakneck romance and a headlong business merger, and almost immediately Ronnie relocated to a condo two towns over where he was tasked with being raucous enough to drive some leaseholders out. Ronnie invited me over, but I never went, and then he and his lady friend moved up to NOVA where foreclosures were all the rage.

A couple with a toddler bought Ronnie's house and immediately tore it down so they could build a new, three-story thing with steel-wire balustrades and tiny triangular windows and landscaping that was chiefly white pebbles dumped from sacks. When they complained about my shaggy trees drooping over their property line, I trimmed them up with the stolen lopper Ronnie had given me way back.

Our little community was famous for a while in a scandalous, sordid way, and people would swing through when they ran TV shows about the killings, mostly trashy rubberneckers with a gloomy bent.

I thought about those women a fair bit, especially Iphigenia Mona Duncan Orestes sprawled in that barn with her bloody hair, but I can't say I ever had much time for the men, the dead ones sticking out of their holes or the live one across the road. Janet bought a new camper van and drove it alone to Nebraska while Casper stayed home and painted their entire house. They've still yet to catch anybody else, so nobody went to jail but the blonde girl who stole a geriatric and a car.

Ruiz and Grimes received commendations at a Lions Club meeting one night. It was a chance for Cliff to make a speech and talk about civic virtues. He had a list of them he displayed with an overhead projector that kept overheating and cutting off. Cliff called Grimes and Ruiz up front and gave them each a jewelry box that had a homely, pewter trinket in it. No engraving. Nothing special. He'd bought them down at the mall and off the shelf.

Grimes insisted on making a thank-you speech, even pulled out his toothpick to do it, and he ended up talking about his daughter who'd died falling down the attic stairs. Grimes went on about how changed he was, how there was a before for him and an after, and then he stopped talking because he could no longer speak.

People will surprise you sometimes, just not nearly often enough.

Ruiz rode with me to Goochland prison one Sunday to pay a call on my mother. I'd bought her a fruitcake because we were crowding Christmas and she'd always liked those things. I knew she'd tell me I shouldn't have. I knew she'd wish we hadn't come. I knew she'd apologize for having ever taken up with my father.

When we were passing through the line and checking in with the guard, I gave him my mother's name and told him, "I'm her son."

"And you?" he asked Ruiz.

I thought she'd pull out her badge and show it, but instead she just said, "I'm his girlfriend, I guess."

We had to wait a while on plastic chairs in a room that was under-heated, and Ruiz saw the Scripture before I did. It was stenciled above a couple of cork boards across the way on the far wall. She gave me a poke. She pointed.

"Book of John," I told her, and Ruiz read it it out like she didn't care who heard.

"'In the world you shall have tribulation,'" she said, "'but be of good cheer. For I have overcome the world.'"

28633872R00139

Made in the USA
Lexington, KY
18 January 2019